OUT OF BODY AND MIND

a novel
by VERONICA JEAN

THE PERMANENT PRESS
Sag Harbor, New York 11963

Copyright © 1993 by Veronica Jean

All rights reserved, including the right to reproduce this book, or parts thereof, in any form, except for the inclusion of brief quotations in a review.

Library of Congress Cataloging-in-Publication Data

Jean, Veronica, 1960–
   Out of body and mind / by Veronica Jean.
     p.   cm.
   ISBN 1-877946-31-1 : $21.95
   I. Title.
PS3560.E18309   1993
813'.54—dc20   92-34343
                                                                    CIP

Manufactured in the United States of America

THE PERMANENT PRESS
Noyac Road
Sag Harbor, NY 11963

*For Bob, my husband, my love, my precious Sandman . . .
Thanks for inviting me over to use your computer.*

Also, I wish to extend my gratitude to all the members of the Downers Grove Writers' Workshop. Especially, Barb, for her inspiration and dedication to helping me untangle the worms.

*A special dedication goes to the memory of
Bill DeBenny, my incestuous love-brother . . .*

Out—out are the lights—out all!
    And, over each quivering form,
The curtain, a funeral pall,
    Comes down with the rush of a storm,
While the angels, all pallid and wan,
    Uprising, unveiling, affirm
That the play is the tragedy, "Man,"
    And its hero the Conqueror Worm.

—Edgar Allan Poe

ONE

It was a paper dream. An art attack. My inside seeping out. The outside seeping in. That's all. No crime on my part. Just art. You might say, the dream went up in smoke. You might say, the joke's on me. But I say, perspective is the artist's most valuable tool.
I don't feel guilty about my role in the inversion of Adam Sault. He was a worm. Many coordinates must fuse for the inversion of one soul. Adam Sault ate a poisoned apple that was delivered by my unsuspecting hand. By most perspectives it appears that Adam Sault was a victim, but the truth is subjective. I ask you, what is truth but one perspective measured by subjective means? I have been found guilty of murder by a jury of my peers; that is one truth. I do not accept guilt as a punishment, and that is another truth. And if a singular truth exists to form the nucleus of this subjective reality I would wager the remainder of my cacophonous thoughts to call it simply, "*Art.*"
I have been sentenced to fifteen years in prison for the premeditated murder of my art teacher, Adam Sault. I don't feel burned by the justice system. The prisoner holds the key. I submit that primal artistic energies are responsible for my theatrical position in this dimension of reality. That's all.
Dr. Marvin (my psychiatrist from back home) would be amazed at how effortlessly I've adapted to prison life. I have my own cell. I keep it clean. It's infinitely small. I have ink drawings of cats and lighthouses taped to the walls. I have a poster I made that reads, **"I DON'T KNOW!"** (Just to remind me.) I write poems and work in the laundry. I eat powdered potatoes and strange kelp-like string beans. I smoke cigarettes, and solicit the affections of other playful women. And time is served, but not observed.

Dr. Marvin said that part of my anxiety disorder was related to my inability to adjust to reality. And I say, he was quite right. My reality was expanding beyond the known parameters at such an accelerated speed that my social adjustment devices began to connect unfamiliar patterns. I became much like outer-space; spilling myself all over the universe.

I've done enough time now to testify that the women in this prison are martyrs, not criminals. Their eyes are shallow and soulless. The moral ghost of guilt sheds very few tears.

There are one hundred-forty-eight multifaceted martyrs here. Rock faces. Ma is the oldest. She says she's sixty-one, but she doesn't look a day over sixty. She's been in and out of various prisons for thirty of the last sixty years. There's not an unlawful bone in her body. She's a scapegoat, like me. She likes to braid my hair. (I have long, straw colored hair, which may be my only remarkable physical feature.) Ma hisses when she laughs. Her front teeth are missing. She has lockjaw, and her teeth were removed so she can eat. Ma names everybody. I'm "Muffin" because I love the corn muffins in here and I have been know to trade *almost* anything for them. My lover is "Pup" because she has big, sad puppy-dog eyes. And she's a bitch.

Lovers don't love each other any more in here than they do on the outside. Dr. Marvin used to say that I was cynical about love because I had poor role models as a child. But I said, "The proof is in the pants, Doc." I said, "You show me a lover, and I'll show you a hard on!"

Dr. Marvin used to say that human beings had the capacity to rationalize anything. He said that I was losing myself in the process of rationalization. But I say, rationalization is one of the intrinsic components of the ego. The ego is creativity unleashed.

I told Dr. Marvin that I believed the evolution of the ego began when Adam and Eve committed that heinous mastication of THE FORBIDDEN FRUIT. And that the real reason they left the garden was not because of their disobedience, but rather because the discovery of the ego beget the insatiable need for a purpose in life. Hence, Adam and Eve busted through the garden wall in search of the real food.

Of course this rationalization process may not have been as apparent to Adam and Eve as it was to Dr. Marvin—as I had told the disbelieving doctor that I was being guided by an entity from another dimension. The entity in question, I call the Sandman. Dr. Marvin did not believe in the Sandman. Dr. Marvin believed in psychological hallucinations.

The Sandman has been my silent guide since I was seven years old, when my father died. The Sandman spoke to me only once, to tell me to deliver the apple to Adam Sault. Dr. Marvin believed that the Sandman was an imaginary father figure I had created out of psychological need. I ask you, what is so unbelievable about a multidimensional entity? I implore you, is it not entirely reasonable to assume that the vast space in which we humans exist should be proliferating entities and energies far beyond the cranial reaches of the imagination?

I was sarcastic to Dr. Marvin. At the time I perceived sarcasm as a defense. I did not begin to understand the depths of my defenses until I unlocked my mind from the vault of singular perceptions.

Pup asks me why I am writing a book. I tell her that it is time to sign my work.

"I don't understand," she says. "What's the book about?"

I tell her, "It's about prison, sort of."

"Am I in it?" she asks.

"We're all in it." I tell her, but she doesn't know what I mean by this.

TWO

I had a public defender at the trial. His name was Randall Perkins. He looked like he worked the two a.m. shift at a donut shop. He had almost invisible skin which stretched over his skeletal frame revealing the web-like map of his pulsing blue veins. He had greasy brown hair. He wiped his sweaty hands off constantly on his navy-blue poly suit. I told him he should grow a beard.
My brother, Robert White, wanted to help me pay for a real lawyer. He's stoic. He's thirty. I'm only twenty-nine. We were born on June 21st exactly one year apart. We are very tight . . . like day and night. Robert works as a bar manager at Eden's Gate, (which is a dank little blues bar near the campus where Adam Sault occasionally imbibed a mug of golden wisdom.) Robert makes less money there than I did when I worked at the cookie factory. Hence, his supportive intentions were overruled by financial reality.

When I'm bored or stir-crazy I have Out of Body Experience. Honest. I can go anywhere. Like a ghost I float right through the concrete walls. Poof! Gone. I had O.B.E. often during the murder trial. Once, when Adam Sault's ex-wife was testifying, I sailed right out of the courtroom. I wandered around the Art Institute for awhile. I like to *hang* inside of "A Sunday Afternoon on the Island of La Grande Jatte" by Georges Seurat. And I pretend I have a parasol and a poofy skirt. I watch the people shuffling up and back trying to fathom all of the dots. Their eyeballs actually sweat.

Art is what got me into this pen. That's the irony I guess. True art has no boundaries. But most people are not artists. They have limitations and immunities. They think art is a substance and not an experience. They keep exotic birds in cages to admire their plumage. I ask you, what is a bird without sky? I implore you, is not the artist the art?

When I came back to my body in the courtroom, Randall Perkins was still questioning Donna Sault, (the ex-wife) and rubbing his hands all over his suit. Donna was a young, trim, forty. She had short frosted hair and mean eyes.

"So, one of your husband's students called you on the phone and claimed she was having an affair with him," Perkins asserted. "Now, would you tell the court how you reacted to this information?"

"I confronted Adam that same evening and he denied it. He said that he had failed that student because she had handed in only one assignment—a still life—she handed in a still life of an apple. He told me that he had nothing to do with her and that she was a disturbed individual."

"Did you believe your husband?"

"No."

"Why not?"

"I was suspicious because he had been working on an art project with me and had suddenly stopped . . . He was working on it at school, he told me . . . but he was coming home later and later each night."

"Did this student contact you again?"

"Yes."

"In what manner did she contact you, Mrs. Sault?"

Donna Sault spoke slowly, yet almost unaffectedly, "She sent me photographs of herself . . . that Adam had taken."

"Nude photographs?" Perkins raised his eyebrows.

"Some of them . . . Yes."

"And what made you certain that your husband was involved with the nude woman in the photos?"

"Because . . . of the designs painted on her skin in the photos . . . that was the project we were working on."

Perkins blinked at her and tipped his head slightly as if he didn't understand. Mrs. Sault added carefully, "He had been photographing me . . . nude, and painting things . . . like animal patterns, spots, and stripes . . ." she sighed, seemingly searching for a word, a thread to tie it up, seal the seam, and get down from the bench, "with acrylic paint. It was Adam's brush work, that was clear."

The girl they were speaking of in the photos was not yours truly. She was a tramp in my drawing class. Her name was Tina-Bend-Me-Over-Tolier. She had a frizzed-out blonde perm and wore tons of black eye makeup. She had zero talent. But she had an alibi. She allegedly was at home with Mrs. Sault at the time the murder was committed. Mrs. Sault and Tina had become friends. They shared the feeble bond of being used for Adam Sault's artistic perversions. (They were tight . . . like gray and white.) Mrs. Sault had let Tina move in with her and also had given her a job at the little picture-framing shop she owned in Lincoln Park.

Tina-B-M-O would swear in court that she had seen me at Eden's Gate at 2:00 a.m. on the night of the murder with a basket of big, shiny, red apples. Tina-B-M-O would also swear that she had not been in contact with Adam Sault for almost a year. (When he dumped her, and she then told his wife about their affair.)

As I listened to this testimony, I became increasingly aware of the bigger picture. I was having greater difficulty with the process of re-entry into the body. I felt safer out there. The universe didn't judge me out there. The creative source of energy seemed to pull me further and further out of my body, and into the cosmos as if to show me how distance changes the entire view.

THREE

Adam Sault was my art teacher. I thought he was attractive. That's all. Besides, I was in therapy with Dr. Marvin for anxiety attacks. The art class was *only* supposed to be a therapeutic exercise.

Dr. Marvin said it was important that I remain unavailable to romantic involvement until I no longer needed therapy. I had promised Dr. Marvin that I would not pursue any relationships until my head was clear and my heart was healed.

In dreams and on paper I would tell Adam Sault how I felt. This was safe.

It Feels Safe

> No one sees you
> Like I do
> You're my Mystery Man.
> I have only a handful
> Of evidence
> About your nature;
> Enough to keep my interest,
> Enough to keep my distance.

When I showed this poem to Dr. Marvin he thought it was clever. He said it was a healthy sign that I was expressing my feelings without fear of criticism. He would swear to this in court.

Dr. Marvin was also attractive. He reminded me of my last five boyfriends who were all tall, dark, bearded, horny, and stupid.

I began seeing the head-doctor because I was hyperventilating at work. I had worked at the cookie factory for the last seven years. I was an oven operator. It was boring. I had a lot of O.B.E. there. One time when I was *Out* I followed a hobo. He had a bottle of wine in a brown paper bag. He stole a pink carnation from a street vendor and brought it to a little old bag lady. She had a cigar and a half-loaf of bread they shared. I burnt the cookies. The whole place was choking on the smoke. I learned not to wander so far on the job.

I was living with BJ when my anxiety affliction began. BJ was instrumental in breaking the boundaries of my heart and propelling me into world of psychiatric intervention.
BJ, a.k.a. Big John, was a gear-head. I met him at the garage one day when my car broke down. He rebuilt my carburetor. He invited me over for dinner the next day. He cooked weinies and beans. We played chess. I let him win. I fell grossly in love with him.
BJ was a pot-head. We used to get stoned, play board games, watch TV and fuck every night. I used to have the joints rolled before he got home from work because he was *temperamental* every day until he smoked.
Big John was six-foot-seven and strong as a pyramid. He was romantic. He sent me roses at the cookie factory for Valentines Day. He made up a game called "find me" by leaving a trail of M&M's through the house. We had mindless fun together. We clung to each other like doughballs to an ungreased cookie sheet—and in the heat of our passion we burned out the chill of loneliness with unspoken promises.
BJ didn't want me to start seeing a shrink. He wanted me all for himself. He said that shrinks made people more neurotic. But the doctor prescribed vitamin V, (Valium) which acted efficiently in slowing down my rapid breathing and it also made me feel like melting, so I went anyway.
The kind, insightful, and attractive doctor asked me what I thought might be causing my anxiety attacks. I said that it was probably because my job was so boring. We spent the first three sessions talking about how boring my job was. I continued to hyperventilate. The doctor increased my dosage of V. When he asked me about BJ, I told him how wonderful he was and how he treated me with total respect and devotion. "So, there's no room for improvement in the relationship?" he asked.

"Well, to be honest, he's a tad on the jealous side," I said. "Too possessive, I guess. You know, he's kind of insecure about my going somewhere without him."

"And how does that make you feel?"

I had heard that question (obliquely) a zillion times in my life, but for the first time it made perfect sense to identify it.

"Smothered," I said. "Not trusted." Long silence . . . "And if you don't have trust in love, then it's not really love—right?"

. . . Long silence. Tears. Kleenexes.

"Have you told John about these feelings?"

"No."

"Why not?"

"Well I just need a little more space, that's all."

"Why don't you put it to him that way? What's the worst that could happen?"

It was my twenty-sixth birthday that day. BJ gave me a pair of diamond earrings. It was the tiniest gift I'd ever received. BJ gloated. I thanked him and fucked him sincerely.

"Honey," I said, holding his monster hands real tight, "I was talking to Dr. Marvin today and he said that I need to tell you how I feel. I love you more than you can know." *The words began to flow like rain down a sewer. This was an ancient ritual, I thought . . . these words have been passed down like archetypes through time . . . and I will say the perfect words . . . and he will understand.* "I will never hurt you or leave you. You've shown me what love really is. But, I need a little more space . . . you know, time for myself, with my friends and stuff. I feel like we have something so strong, but I just feel like you don't trust me sometimes. So I don't do some of the things I really want to do cause I'm afraid you'll think I don't want to be with you. And I just need for you to trust me a little more. Trust my love."

I leaned over and kissed his beard and tried to hug him, but he just lay there and stared right past me.

Long silence.

"Honey, hello in there," I said, putting my face right in front of his and smiling real goofy.

He looked disgusted.

"Honey, please talk to me," I begged. "Please, this is so important."

Dead silence.

[15

"C'mon, tell me what you're thinking, BJ, baby," I whined. "C'mon, this is supposed to be a sharing relationship."

Then he looked at me with a look that could frost the sun, and lunged out of the room. I sat on the bed and started sobbing. I groveled into the living room where he was sitting in the dark. I knelt down on the floor and buried my head in his lap. "I'm sorry," I cried. "Just talk to me, John. TALK TO ME! I can't handle the silence."

"If you can't handle it," he spat, "you know where the door is." He pushed me away and went back into the bedroom. I sobbed louder and followed him in there.

"Don't do this, John. Oooh,Ug,Ug,Waaah!" I sounded like a clogged sewer pipe, "Pleese,Ug,Ug . . ."

"You need more space," he said bitterly, "there's the door. I want you out by tomorrow."

I ran back out onto the couch and smashed my slobbering face into a pillow. I wailed on for an hour or so. Then I thought that if I got real quiet, he'd come out after me. But he didn't.

Some birthday.

I didn't leave the next day. I stayed home from work and cried into a bucket to see if I could fill it with tears. I took five Valiums and fell asleep. I dreamt about BJ opening the apartment door and water gushing around him as I floated, face down in a lucid pool of tears. And as the tears rushed out the door, my body was sucked to the floor. All I could hear was BJ squishing across the carpet, and then kneeling down to weep over my soggy soul.

BJ apologized when he came home. I didn't have to show him the bucket of tears. He said that he did trust me and he always would. We smoked a joint, fucked, and we were happy as ginger snaps again.

One night, two weeks later, I was making his favorite weinies and beans. I was whistling in the kitchen when BJ stormed into the apartment all red in the face. I forgot to roll the joints!

"OUT!" he hollered, as he opened the door and started throwing my stuff into the hallway.

I responded to this subtle gesture. *OK, buddy, I can take a hint.*

I guzzled my pride and retreated to the eternally open door of my faithful brother, Robert.

"I told you the guy was a jerk," Robert said. (He said this about every man I was attracted to.) "Jesus, Eve, you only knew him three weeks when you moved in with him. What did you expect?"

Robert said that men would never give me the respect I deserved because I was "romantically delusional."

But I say, romantic delusions are just one of the germ cells which produce the zygote of art, and the pure artist possesses no immunities against such germs.

Dr. Marvin said that my relationship with BJ was foul and imbalanced, and that it would take courage for me to understand and confront the issues that were causing my anxiety. But I was emotionally dismembered. My heart crumbled like a burnt cookie as I thought about Big John. How could he profess love for me one day and start heaving my stuff out the door the next? What was this pain that had no name? Why was I so dizzy all the time? Why was I taking more V's then the doctor prescribed? Why did I ask so many questions? Was there a plan in the universe for me? Was there a design to life, or did my ego merely create the fantasy, the illusion out of rationalization?

The poster in my cell reminds me; **"I DON'T KNOW!"**

FOUR

"What time's it?" P.J. asks every guard that passes. "What time's it?"
 The guards banter, "Why, do you have an appointment or something?"
 Eleven o'clock.
 Eleven fifteen.
 Eleven thirty.
 Lights out.
 P.J. has the cell next to mine. When she isn't asking what time it is, she's asking "Gotta extra smoke?"
 THERE ARE NO EXTRA SMOKES IN HERE! She smokes constantly and furiously. Her teeth are black. She is black. She spends her toothpaste and shampoo money on cigarettes. She's been here for over five years and she has earned no privileges. She has had no lovers. Her nose is smashed flat and she has a sad, half-moon scar under her left eye. She never talks about why she's here, just, "What time's it? Gotta smoke?"
 Five and a half years ago Pamela Jenkins (P.J.) was featured on the front page of every major newspaper in the Chicago area under the headline "WOMAN STABS HUSBAND TO DEATH; PLEADS SELF DEFENSE." The jury found her guilty of first degree manslaughter. She stabbed him seventy-two times. She said, "He just kept comin' at me."
 I say, she's inculpable. I ask you, is a river guilty for flooding if it rains too much? She had to defend herself. He kept coming at her.
 I asked P.J. why she always wanted to know the time and she replied, "Time is the only thing I can count on."
 I have this theory about "doing time": The only time I can experience *physically* is the present, I can fill this time with

wonder or I can miss the moment altogether by being anxious or nostalgic.

Out of Body time however, is in another dimension. A parallel dimension, if you will, where the substance of time is inverted into energy via black holes in space. Honest.

P.J. listens imperviously to my theories about time and black holes. She says, "I don't think any of that shit matters."

"What does matter?" I ask her.

"Food," she replies. "If you grew up as hungry as I did, you'd know—that's a fact."

"What about being here," I probe, "what about being in prison?"

"What about it?" She glares at me with the ebony daggers in her eye sockets. I can see the bloody knife cracking through my rib cage and lunging into my heart over and over till I am mutilated like her husband.

"Well," I say, "I did grow up hungry. My parents were both drunks and there was never enough—of anything." I sigh, "Food is essential, P.J., you're right . . . but I don't know if it's the only essential."

"Gotta extra smoke?" she asks.

I shake one out of my pack and pass it to her.

She nods and walks off to smoke in the filmy-yellow haze of the wreck-room. There is a bellowing TV in the wreck-room, its electric colored micro-dots flash incessant advertisements for frosty white teeth and luminous hair; for frothy champagne and fat cheeseburgers; for blue jeans that make buns look like happy cantaloupes. The commercials tell us there are people standing in line to own pocket-sized automobiles that comfortably accommodate two beaming adults, two respectful offspring, and an obedient schnauzer all for only a few thousand dollars. The commercials tell us a lot of things that have nothing to do with our reality.

P.J. gazes privately at the TV. She doesn't seem interested or provoked by the mouth-watering-aromatic-gooey-rich food commercials. She doesn't seem attached to anything but the cigarette she sucks on like a tit. She reminds me of my mother. She reminds me of my mother who stared drunkenly at the TV, while she, my brother, and I waited for the ambulance to come and take away my dead dad.

There is another dimension inside the television. A dimension where everything is resolved. A dimension of abundance. A dimension where P.J. and Pup could work in an antiseptic hospital, wearing white nurses uniforms and flirting with young, bushy-eyebrowed doctors, instead of being prison junkies. A dimension where my brother could be a witty, late night talk show host, instead of being a sociopathic misfit. A dimension where Dr. Marvin could save patients with acute anxiety disorders. A dimension where my mother could star in movies with Elvis Presley and have her own line of cosmetics, instead of drinking herself into a state of inertia. A dimension where fiction is the source of energy, which in turn propels the soul into the corridor where all the doors open. Imagine that.

FIVE

Dr. Marvin had asked me to define my relationship with my mother. "I don't know," I said. (I said this a lot in the beginning of therapy, and have since returned to that enlightened observation.) "My mother is a good-hearted woman. She means well. She just wasn't the P.T.A. type."
"Are you defending her?"
"What do you mean defending her?"
"Well, you told me before that your mother ignored you."
"She had a lot of responsibilities after my dad died."
"Like staying drunk?"
"She drank a lot," I stated flatly.
"How does that make you feel?"
"I don't know. She made sure we always had a roof over our heads."
"And cold cereal for supper," Dr. Marvin retorted.
FUCK YOU. I'm thinking, just FUCK YOU! Just what do you know about hard times Buddy? What do you know about having a battered drunk as a role model? A woman who dragged her ass home every night with her make-up sliding off her face, smelling like rancid beer and stale cigarettes—staggering from the painful calluses and blisters on her feet from working twelve hours a day as a waitress at a goddamn greasy-spoon. JUST WHAT THE FUCK DO YOU KNOW?
I stared at Dr. Marvin. He thinks he's real smart. He wears sincere suits. He probably pays thirty-five dollars for a haircut. I smile.
"We had turkey almost every Thanksgiving," I said smugly.

Food is essential to my story. It becomes increasingly clearer to me that I have limited control of my role in the food chain. The big fish eat the little fish, the cats eat the birds, the worms eat the apples, and that is just part of the

[23

system of inversion. The body feeds upon the mind. And if the mind is filled with venomous thoughts, then the body will respond accordingly. The body has a perfect system for inverting food and thought into energy. The mind, however, as a part of the body which believes it is independent of the system, is as meddlesome as a ravenous child. The mind wants to master the macrocosm. The mind has the power to consume the soul that creates it.

Women in prison are beyond consumption. They are hungry for everything; inside and out. Women in prison are not bona fide lesbians. It is more a social order which evolves out of loneliness, humility, and desperation for understanding. (And of course, rationalization.) In fact, most of the women here have been sentenced for crimes of passion. They loved their men beyond the recommended parameters of human intimacy, beyond the fuzzy-wuzzy kisses, beyond the roses and the poetry, beyond the sweaty grinding rituals; they loved their lovers to death.

My playmate, Pup, thinks she's tough. She is hungry for attention. One day she stands up in the mess hall and yells "ALPO!" at the top of her lungs and whips her plate of "Scum-Suey" at a guard. But it hits Barney upside the head. (Barney is a woman who looks like Barney Rubble on the Flintstones cartoon show.) Barney then flings her whole tray in Pup's general direction and it's a free-for-all. P.J. and I duck and keep eating. Pup goes to solitary for awhile. Those of us with detail privileges get to clean up the mess. Imagine that.

When Pup gets out of "the hole" she comes to me. Crying. "I can't take it anymore Muffin. Waaaahh! I just can't take it. I swear I'd sell my left tit for a T-bone steak! A pizza! A fucking milk shake!" I hold her like a baby while she shakes and snivels. I tell her I love her, even though she doesn't know what I mean by this. She's not at all like the men I used to fall for. She's not tall, dark, bearded, horny or stupid. She's contemptuous. That's all.

Dr. Marvin suggested that part of my anxiety disorder was due to repressing my sexuality by getting involved with the same type of domineering men over and over. He thought I had "desires" for my best friend, Jooly Jones. He thought I had "desires" for my brother. He thought a lot about sex and I recommended that maybe he ought to see a therapist about his preoccupation.

Dr. Marvin said that my submissive sexual roles were unhealthy and that lust had greater powers over me than I understood. That may have been true then, but today I say, sexuality is an overrated mystique. Sexuality is neutral in the universe. It serves our nature most appropriately until we personify it. When humans complicate matters which are simple, then they give power to myths. And I say, whatever myths we shall worship or fear shall in turn imprison our souls.

SIX

My soul sister, Jooly Jones, is a god-send. (If you believe in that sort of thing.) We are very tight, like left and right. We've been best friends since the fifth grade. She lived in a ranch house on my street. Her parents were old. They had shiny furniture and two color TV sets. Her brothers and sisters were all away in college.

Jooly Jones and I became friends when she stuck up for me one day when some kids in school were making fun of my ratty clothes. We walked home together from school that day and she said, "People are vain and ignorant, but don't worry about it, cause it all evens out in the end. Rude people are reincarnated as earthworms in their next lives and used for fish bait."

"Bullshit!" I said.

"Really, my sister told me all about that stuff. Why should I lie?"

"Why does anybody lie?"

"Really, if you want to know when I'm lying, you can tell cause my left eye starts twitching."

As she says this of course, her left eye is twitching. "O.K. fish food it is," I say.

Jooly Jones was cool. She used to invite me over for lunch in the summer. Mrs. Jones would make flying-saucer-shaped grilled cheese sandwiches and serve us tall glasses of cold milk on the back porch. Jooly had a zillion stuffed animals in her bedroom. Her walls and ceiling were plastered with posters of Mick Jagger. She'd strut right up and lick one of the posters and go, "Yeah! Mick, someday you and me babe!" She told me that Mick was androgynous, and what that meant. And in 1970 when I was still wearing Salvation Army "flood pants," she *gave* me a pair of her big bell-bottomed, bona fide, Levi Strauss blue-jeans.

Jooly was precocious. We built a tree fort in the woods nearby in the summer of sixth grade. We had pocket knives. We smoked cigarettes. We called ourselves The Women's Anti-gravity Association. Jooly hung a sign on the door that said: NO BOYS WITH PENISES ALLOWED INSIDE!

My brother, Robert, was jealous. He had always been my number one playmate. He started hanging around with a rapacious beast-boy named Ernie Stone. Ernie had a wrist-rocket slingshot. He and Robert started killing little animals and birds and leaving the stiff bodies scattered at the trunk of our tree.

Jooly said, "It's a primitive offering. Sort of like the young male Neanderthal having to prove his skills as a hunter before a female will mate with him. I vote we let them in the club. If we can direct their juvenile energies away from killing innocent beasts, then perhaps we can make use of their hunting skills."

So we let Ernie and Robert join us and we became The Cosmic Cat Council. Jooly said, "Cats are the coolest cause they have nine lives. So between the four of us we'll have thirty-six and we'll get away with murder!"

We all told our parents that we were staying over at each other's houses one night. We pooled our resources to camp out at the club. Robert and I brought some Twinkies and Oreo cookies. Ernie stole four cans of beer from home. Jooly hit the jackpot, her ultra-coolest sister gave her a nickel-bag of marijuana.

It was a steamy August night. The clubhouse swirled with sweet smelling, sticky smoke. A full moon rolled lazily across the thick sky like a bloated beachball. The universe was wheezing. We laughed till our teeth hurt. Then we howled like ravenous pack-dogs, our delirious echoes rippling through the cosmic orb. Robert said we should become blood brothers and sisters. Jooly and I took out our pocket knives and carefully cut everyone's thumbs. We sat in a tight circle and pressed our thumbs together till blood ran down our arms. Then Robert said, "Together forever, through wrong and right; The Cosmic Cats are as tight as day and night!" We each took a drink from the same can of beer.

SEVEN

It was during the peak days of The Cosmic Cat Council's sinister summer, that I fully understood the implications of synchronistic inversion. We had committed our innocent little minds to the devious mission of spinning our tranquil suburban backdrop into a territory where children and other whimsical creatures could have a little fun.

We invented the coolest game of all called, "Twilight Zoning." The object of the game was to amuse ourselves by creating situations which would leave people in a state of total doubt. Which we called "Zoned."

Ernie Stone, our B.B.B. (Brilliant Blood Brother) invented the game when he suggested to the C.C.C. one day, "You know what would be really cool . . ." *He stared us all down with his beady-eyed, brat-face.* "What if we went over to Fairlanes Apartments and switched the license plates on all the cars?"

We squealed with impish delight and agreed to execute the Zoning that same evening.

The next day we walked through Fairlanes individually, so as not to attract attention. What we witnessed was a BONA FIDE ZONE-O-CARNIVAL! People were strutting around, bobbing up and down, and clucking like chickens. Policemen stood by, worthlessly tapping their pens on little notebooks.

This artful-harvest had sprouted genius seeds for our future misadventures. With the stealth and fearlessness which only the coolest of cats could conjure up, we pounced on the little town of Maplewood, Illinois.

We used Ernie's father's wheel barrow and silently borrowed twenty-two Virgin Mary statues from the combined front lawns of Birch, Elm and Green Streets and set them up to scrimmage on the High School football field. And we Zoned the good people of Oak Street by unscrewing one side of their mailboxes (the kind attached to the wall by the front door) and then we left the screw inside the box for them to screw it back in. If the house numbers were wrought iron plates (as many of them were in our neighborhood) we switched the numbers around. We did not soap their windows. We did not T.P. their trees. We set their lawn sprinklers up on their roofs so they would think it was raining.

Jooly Jones and I were on our way to a pay telephone one Thursday afternoon to execute a dime-scam, (A dime-scam is when you ask a stranger if they'll trade you a dime for ten pennies; they will invariably give you the dime and tell you to keep your pennies.) (Note: This does not work in prison.) when Jooly saw a sight she could not bear. In the alley next to someone's garbage cans lay a Cuddly Duddly with a broken neck.

Cuddly Duddly was a bright orange, **long necked**, stuffed, talking dog on "The Ray Rayner Show." (A morning TV show for children.) Cuddly Duddly was dopey. Every morning he talked to us in his dopey-puppy voice and read letters from kids who had written to the show just to hear their names on TV. But dopey as he was, Cuddly Duddly was above all *severely* cuddly. Hundreds of kids received these lifesized, (about three feet tall) endearing, stuffed animals for Christmas presents. But due to a flaw in the construction of Cuddly Duddly, by summertime most of them had broken necks.

Jooly grabbed the dead Cuddly up in her arms and brought it back to the clubhouse. We performed surgery. We made an incision at the neck seam and inserted a wire coat hanger to give his neck stability. We stuffed newspapers and rags around the hanger and then sewed him back up. Then we brushed his orange fur till he looked dopey and optimistic again.

A week later Ernie Stone delivered another dilapidated dog to the clubhouse. In addition to a broken neck, this one had no eyes. A mission was in order. Cuddly Deadly would return from beyond to Zone the careless owner who threw him away.

We stuffed the deadly doggie's busted neck and painted the stitches red. We glued on bloodshot ping-pong balls for eyes. We filled his mouth with shaving cream and matted his fur with rubber cement.

Jooly, Robert and I, perched in the trees so we could witness the Zoning. Ernie Stone tiptoed up to the dark house on Pine street where he had found the broken beast. He placed Cuddly Deadly in the center of the porch. He looked around. He knocked on the door three times LOUD. He bolted. He wasn't ten feet across the front yard when the porch light went on and a huge black dog barreled out of the house. Ernie zig-zagged across the lawn. We leapt from the trees and pulled out our pocket knives. Ernie cut towards the alley. The dog closed in on him. We closed in on the dog.

When Ernie hit the alley, inversion hit Ernie. Inversion in the form of a black Ford Pick-up Truck, flying down the alley with no headlights on. Ernie flew up in the air like a bowling pin. The truck crashed into a garage. The dog ran away.

I stopped breathing.

Robert stopped breathing.

Jooly screamed.

Our B.B.B. lay next to the garbage cans with a busted neck.

Dr. Marvin said that what happened to our B.B.B. was tragic. He said that the C.C.C. stage was something that all juvenile delinquents go through, and that I was lucky to have not ended up doing heroin or doing time in a detention center.

Jooly Jones and I came to many conclusions after Ernie's inversion and we spent more time together pondering the inconceivable nature of energy.

My brother, Robert, after the Zoning, detached from Jooly's and my senseless pursuits. He remained mute for several months until one day, when he found a guitar in someone's garbage. The guitar, from that point on, was my brother's voice. A shrill, electric wail, I suppose, is better than no voice at all.

EIGHT

Jooly Jones got me my job at the cookie factory. We were nineteen then. She gave me a tour of the factory. It smelled like heaven. (I believed then that heaven was a place of peak sensual awareness.) She then handed me a red apron with the cookie man logo on it and said, "I get to train you, Pal, and you're gonna love it. Today we're baking chocolate chip crumbs cause the dough-boy fucked up and put in too much corn starch, so they break apart as soon as they cool. Then we get to throw them away."

I grinned and socked her in the arm. "It's a crummy job but somebody's gotta do it!"

She laughed, "You catch on quick, Eve, and we'll make a baker outta you in no time."

She told me about the "little rat problem" at the factory. "We have several, very fat, Rat-Cats here, still make sure you check your oven thoroughly between every cool-down. BURNING RAT STINKS!"

I found a rat in my oven once. It stared at me from the dark corner of the oven with tears in its beady black eyes. Its little whiskers trembled with fear as it begged me for mercy. I chased it with a broom into a stock cookie box and set it free outside. Jooly said I should be canonized.

Eight years later Jooly Jones would swear in court that I was competent and dependable as a fellow employee. That I was loyal as a friend. And that I was so passive, I couldn't even kill a rat.

The first time she came to see me in prison she said, "Why'd you do it Eve? Just tell me. I'm your best friend. You know I'll understand."

I grinned and socked her in the arm. "It was a crummy job but somebody had to do it."

Dr. Marvin asked me if I had any *special* feelings for Jooly. Dr. Marvin thought that I was suppressing what he implied was a natural bonding among females. He asked me if I ever wanted to touch Jooly.

"What're you asking Doc? Why don't you just be straight with me?"

"All right. I'm just wondering, since you speak so highly of Jooly . . . if you aren't seeking her affection to replace John?"

Dr. Marvin wanted everything to be complicated. I wanted everything to be simple. "She's my best friend and I love her. That's all." I answered.

"Like a sister?"

"I guess."

"Like your brother?"

Like my brother! Fish food I'm thinking. Dr. Marvin wants to be fish food in his next life.

He was convinced that I had some sort of incestuous desire for my brother. He was wrong. I love my brother like a brother. No other brother could take his place. That's all.

Dr. Marvin thinks that love is an addiction. But I say, pure love is the only cure for addiction. When pure love is experienced the whole universe becomes fused with the addict and hence, there is no illusion to attain; there is no need to get high for she is already transcendent of the highest high. Honest.

NINE

Dr. Marvin wanted to know all about the string of lovers I was involved with before I met Big John. I told him they all came from the same *mold*. They all had various addictions. They all had dark hair, eyes and beards. They all looked like my father, who looked like Jesus Christ, who looked like God. (Or so I postulated at that time.) They all used me up and tossed me out like a broken toy, with the exception of Rodger Badger.

Rodger Badger was my lover before Big John. We met at Roots, a reggae bar in Chicago. Rodger was dark. Rodger was Jamaican.

The bar was swirling thick with that sweet smelling, sticky smoke which Jamaicans are so fond of. I was gazing deeply into the bottom of my green beer bottle when this profound creature danced into my peripheral view. He was a-swayin' his arms and a-bendin' his knees like a bona fide Rastafarian. His mop of dreadlocks swung to and fro like seaweed in shimmering tidepool. He was shirtless and sleek with sweat. I wanted to touch his bony body. I wanted to taste his salty tears. I wanted to know such inner rhythm. I wanted to jam with this Neanderthal man!

We spent a lot of time at Roots. Rodger worked for the band that played there, though I'm not sure what his job was. We smoked a lot. We danced a lot. We kissed a lot. We gazed into each others eyes a lot. Jooly and I shared an apartment together at that time and we had made a deal with each other that,"NO BOYS WITH PENISES ARE ALLOWED IN-SIDE," except on the weekends. So we did not fuck a lot.

I asked Rodger Badger a zillion questions. I knew that he knew the meaning of life. But Rodger was oblique. Like a zen zombie he would put his hand on my breast and say "Inner rhythm cannot be sought, it can only be found."

And I would ask, "Well, golly Rog', then how do I find it?"

And Rog' would kiss me and say, "It finds you."

Rodger Badger was not in love with me. He was in love with the universe. His eyes were always glassy and half closed. He saw only one truth.

I tried to open his eyes. "Rog', look at me" I said. I was tracing his protruding ribs with my fingers. "I care about you a lot. You don't seem to care about anything. I mean what if I got sick or something? What if you got sick? I mean life is real, buddy, and you're just lettin' it pass you by. Look at me." There was a distance deep beneath the glass spheres in his eye sockets, a distance I longed to reach. "I love you Rodger. Isn't that something? Isn't love at least a worthwhile pursuit?"

"Eve, I do love you," he smiled proudly. "But you don't understand. Yet. True love is goalless. My only goal in life is to become goalless."

Six days after that deep conversation, Rodger Badger died of a heroin overdose. Life was an insurmountable obstacle in his pursuit of goallessness.

I told Dr. Marvin that my relationship with Rodger was the least significant of all my love excursions because it only lasted three months, two weeks, and six and a half days.

Dr. Marvin asked me how long after Rodger died had I met Big John.

"Twenty-seven days Doc, but it was different because BJ and I were madly in love with each other right from the start. We had rapport. We had commitment. We had fun!"

"So you don't think you were desperate for love?"

"Doctor, I don't think you know a damn thing about love, or passion, or what makes chemistry between two people."

"But I'm not the one who's suffering from acute anxiety Eve, you are. And I know enough about human nature to know that when people act out of desperation it's because they are driven by fear. You feared being alone so much that you accepted John's invitation without even considering that he might be as desperate as you."

Dr. Marvin believes that the root of all emotions can be traced to either fear or love. But I say, fear and love are the friction that puts fire in the heart. That's all.

TEN

After BJ tossed me out like an old tomato, I started taking my therapy sessions a little more seriously. (I also started taking vitamin V a little more seriously.) I admitted to Dr. Marvin that I felt lost. I couldn't bear the thought of having my heart squashed ever again.

I had been involved in five fatal relationships in the last six years. Every one of them with men like BJ, men like my father, men like Dr. Marvin, men who were about as sensitive to my feelings as a worm is to an apple that it devours from the inside out.

I told Dr. Marvin that I didn't know why I fell in love with men who took advantage of my good nature. He said that I needed to dig deep into the feelings I had as a child. I said, "I don't think that my childhood was very meaningful."

"What do you feel a meaningful childhood consists of?" he asked.

"I don't know. I guess if I had excelled at something at an early age, then I might have a stronger sense of purpose today."

He asked if my parents had encouraged me academically.

I laughed. "My school work was bad enough, I didn't need their intellectual involvement to make it worse."

He asked me what my father was like.

"I don't remember," I said closing my eyes.

"You seem to have a selective memory loss, Eve."

... Long silence ...

I looked straight into the doctor's deep-dark eyes, "I think my father was evil," I said severely.

"What do you mean by evil?" he asked.

"I mean there was something wicked under his skin. Something terrifying that twisted his thoughts. Something that he

couldn't escape from and something that he couldn't face because he couldn't even see it."
"Did your father hurt you?"
"No, he was just evil."
"Did your father ever hurt you Eve?"
"No . . . He hurt my mother."

When Dad finished building the recreation room, with the huge bar and the huge fireplace, he threw a huge party. Robert and I were only five and six years old so we had to go to bed at ten o'clock.

I woke up in the middle of the night when I heard yelling and glass breaking. I went into Robert's room and woke him.

"I think Mom and Dad are fighting," I said, "come out there with me."

We stood by the doorway in our footy-pajamas holding hands. Dad was behind the bar. Mom was on the floor, bleeding. Dad was throwing glasses and bottles at her. We stood there frozen till Dad saw us and yelled, "GO BACK TO YOUR ROOMS!"

We both started crying. Then Mom looked up and yelled,"GET BACK INTO BED NOW!"

We went back to our rooms and sobbed our little eyeballs out. It got quiet all of a sudden. I closed my eyes real tight and waited for the next crash. I waited and waited. I shivered. I thought Dad had killed Mom. I was standing with my ear pressed up against the door, and suddenly, POOF! I was in the hallway. Everything was porous and appeared to be made of glowing micro-dots. I felt weightless, like a bubble. I spun around. I could see the bedroom door was still closed and in between the glowing micro-dots, I saw my body like a silhouette still pressed up against the door. I soared down the hallway and burst right through the wall into the rec-room. Mom was crying, her mouth agape in a silent scream. A stream of blood trickled out of her nose and mingled orange with her tears. Dad was pulling her hair and humping her like an animal. I flew back to my body with revolting shame. I collapsed and prayed to God that my dad would die.

Dr. Marvin doesn't believe in O.B.E.
Dr. Marvin believes in psychosis.

The dapper doctor deduced that my need to be involved with men like BJ was directly related to the guilt I felt for wishing my father would die. He said that my whole family was living an illusion and that I could no longer tell what was real and what was a projection of my mental desires.

I said, "Is it wrong to deceive myself?"

"It's not right or wrong, Eve. It's a matter of whether you've made the choice yourself."

"I see," I said, but I truly did not see.

In fact I don't think I began to see any possibilities until I began writing poetry. The doors began to open then. The doors began to creak slowly open and a faint beam of moon-mist dusted through my brain. Distinction! Words were the missing keys to my vast warehouse of art. Words were the source of the energy. Words would put the pieces of the puzzle together. Words would bridge the immense distance between thought and feeling.

Don't Ask Me Why

At the open air market
    I bought a big red apple
its meat was so sweet and juicy
    it dribbled down my chin.
Don't ask me why,
    it reminded me of you.

At the laundromat
    I watched an old black man.
His flat shoes shuffled
    as he folded fluffy towels.
Don't ask me why,
    it reminded me of you.

At the edge of the water
    where the moon's echo trembled
I listened to a song
    it was distant but familiar.
Don't ask me why,
    it reminded me of you.

Dr. Marvin asked me what was the significance of the laundromat in the poem. I said that I wanted to show myself in a place where "dirty 'emotional' laundry" gets cleaned-up.

"That's very clever, Eve. I think you should keep writing. You seem to be gaining some insight to your emotional struggles."

I winked, "I just want to be *right* Doc."

He increased my dosage of Valium.

Ma, the sage old crone here in prison, says that shrinks are really repressed maniacs. She thays, between her mithing two front teeth, that, "Shrinkth are thothially maladjusthted freaksth, and they are drawn into sthychiatry becausth their twisthted egoths thrive upon feeling sthuperior to the sthick persthonalitiesth that they compare themthelvesth to."

I told her that Dr. Marvin helped me heal my tattered heart and he also helped me free my spirit to explore my artistic reality and fuse with the universe.

She hissed long and loud, "SSSSS! He alstho helped you right into pristhon, Sthweetie! SSSSS!"

I say, it is not imperative that anyone agrees with the artist, but she must agree implicitly with herself.

ELEVEN

There are several women here who call themselves artists. It is not imperative that I agree with them. They don't consider their crimes a form of art as I do. They have killed, robbed, or otherwise broken rules primarily out of greed. However, I must learn to consider the viability that greed is, indeed, a popular form of art.

There are several women here who write poetry. They are depressing.

There are several women here who don't know how to read. They are lucky.

I read to Pup from the books that my brother Robert, and other compassionate souls, like Jooly Jones, donate to the prison library. Pup likes Stephen King the best. She thinks he is funny. I think he's not boring.

Prison is boring.

Prison is depressing.

But I say, prison is a perspective observed solely by victims of martyrdom.

St. Birdy is a victim of martyrdom. We call her "Birdy" because she sings majestically. She sings unearthly songs which transcend our grim experience. She sings pure to the core of spiritual inversion. (She mostly sings Elvis and Beatles songs, but any music in prison is a remarkable gift.) In fact, I can hear her now, three cells down . . . "Ah-look-at-all-the-lone-ly-peep-ul . . ." She doesn't know all of the words and she will repeat any given refrain for hours. She has learned to fluctuate the melody to avoid beatings from inmates who cannot tolerate the repetition.

We call her Saint because of the nature of her incarceration. Birdy was busted for stealing and possibly burying the body of St. Innocentius. There is no evidence to indicate where the body might be buried. The ground was frozen in Chicago that time of year, but Birdy insists that she, "Returned it to the earth."

St. Birdy, a.k.a. Robyn Perkins, was seen leaving the Mayslake Franciscan Retreat in Oak Brook, Illinois, on December 21st, 1987, with the body of the canonized boy, St. Innocentius. She had visited the monks' retreat earlier that day with her women's choir ensemble to sing Christmas songs. Their group was given a tour of the grounds and led through the various chambers of the immaculate order. Then, they were taken to the chapel where Robyn Perkins would discover her role in the bigger picture of cosmic inversion.

The boy saint was laid out in a glass case with a red velvet curtain draped around it. The Brother who had guided their tour said that Saint Innocentius had found his home here and would rest in eternal peace with the prayers of the Brothers. A framed, poorly typed, photocopy of a biography of St. Innocentius hung on the wall above the shrine. It claimed that the body of this child was found in the catacombs. It didn't say why the child was canonized, only that he was presumed to be around seven years old at the time of his death.

When the Brother pulled open the velvet drape, Robyn Perkins gasped in horror. The child lay there in a dainty white lace gown. Its hands and feet were wearing gold mesh mittens and booties through which you could see the shrivelled up skin and tiny bones. On the head was a grotesque open-eyed doll mask with long black synthetic hair. Robyn felt Zoned. She looked at the other women in the group who were awed to be in the presence of a true saint. Their heads were bowed offering prayer. And Robyn heard a tiny bell-like, lisping voice whisper in her ear, "Help me. Thet me free. My thpirit will not athcend until I am returned to the earth."

Robyn left quietly with the others but that night she returned. She busted the glass case with a tire iron and wrapped the crumbling body in her winter coat. Then she zoomed out of the building. But one of the Brothers saw her as she ran down the dark corridor and scrambled into her car. He gave the police her license plate number but she was not apprehended for several days.

She pleaded not guilty, and because of her brother, (a.k.a.; the public defender at my trial,) Randall Perkins' expertise in criminal defense she was only sentenced to a maximum of ten years. She committed this heinous abomination when she was only nineteen and the Honorable Judge declared that there would be no appeal for probation unless the defendant would disclose the location of the missing corpse.

Case closed.

Birdy doesn't sing for worms.

TWELVE

The world was wriggling with twisted worms. The dirt was beginning to slide in around me. I had been in therapy with Dr. Marvin for six months. My mental condition was deteriorating. I was despondent. I was lethargic. I was taking eighty or a hundred milligrams of vitamin V a day. There was nothing to strive for. The love in my heart had fizzled out like a wet firecracker. No boom. No bang. Not even a tiny pop. I was wrong. There was no such thing as romantic love. It was a childish dream. That's all. I never loved Big John and he never loved me. We loved each other's bodies with no passion or depth that could reach the souls.

Dr. Marvin encouraged me in therapy. Robert placated me at home. Jooly Jones tried to cheer me up at work. "Look at you, Eve," she would shake me gently by the shoulders. "You look anorexic. Your clothes are hanging on you like trash bags. You wear that stupid red Budweiser cap every day, no make-up, and workboots. The guys here think you're a dyke."

"So what Jooly, I think they're boring."

"So, there's a vast, beautiful sea of men out there. But if you're ever gonna catch a big one you've gotta get your line back in the water."

I could feel a lump bulging in my throat and my eyes starting to burn. "Jooly," I said gravely, "I don't want to be fish food anymore. It hurts too much when you get chewed up and spit back out. It hurts too much when the magic carpet unravels and you wake up on the cold, hard floor of truth. It hurts too much to look in the mirror and realize that this hollow shell is all that anyone can see." One lonely tear spilled from my eye and trickled slowly down my cheek where it dangled, and then simply let go, splattering itself into a zillion desolate particles on the cookie factory floor.

"OK, so you're depressed about John. I understand. I've been dumped before too. But it's been six months now. It's time for you to snap out of it. You never would have been happy with him. Remember? He smothered you. You deserve better than that Eve. A lot better."

"Oh, sure Jooly, it's easy for you to say. You're busy humping MR-I'LL-LOVE-YOU-TILL-THE-DAY-I-DIE-AND-EVEN-THEN-MY-LOVE-WILL-JUST-BEGIN-TO-GROW-JOE-PERFECT! When are you gonna wake up Jooly? Who's the fishy in the brook? You are, and he's got you hooked."

So I was a little jealous. That's all.

It was Dr. Marvin who suggested that I take an art class at the college night school program. He said it would be therapeutic for me to get involved in a controlled social environment. He also said that many of his patients found art to be cathartic and that they developed new levels of awareness to their innermost feelings.

I agreed to take a drawing class. I did not intend to purge my hidden feelings on paper. I intended to endure it until I woke up from this ignominious nightmare. But Adam Sault inverted my intentions. The moment I saw the need in Adam Sault's forgiving eyes I was altered. I was not fully aware of my feelings at that moment (as Dr. Marvin was so adept at pointing out) but on the edge of my expanding reality I was conscious of a faint ember in my heart for Adam Sault.

Dr. Marvin was curious. He asked me why this drawing class seemed to spark my interest in poetry.

I knew that Dr. Marvin would have something stupid to say if I told him that I had a *crush* on my art teacher so I cleared my throat and said real seriously, "I think that drawing is teaching me the value of values. I feel an overwhelming desire to individualize and expound upon my drawings. Poetry seems to clarify the nebulous subjects that we dare to call art. That's all."

Dr. Marvin said that I was making progress.

But I say, progress is an illusion. When energy is used to produce an intended progression, then the existing energy bank will regress. Hence, it will draw from other energy sources producing a perpetual regression in the progress of all interrelated energies.

Adam Sault was just a vehicle, I told myself. Just a tool for carving a sculpture. Just a line that linked me to the interrelated energies of art. Just a line in a vast drawing, which was becoming the portrait of my life.

My life until the poetry began had been a mere outline. A thin black string of silhouettes that mocked my vision of love. A thin black string that I swallowed because it was there in my throat, like a worm. And the more I swallowed the more I realized there was no end. The string is out there tied to everything and I'm trying to consume it all—roll it all up into a neat ball. It forms a lump in my throat till I can't breathe. It ties knots in my brain. It weaves garments of words to conceal the naked pain of the heart. It builds walls to imprison the soul, within the mind.

Building

>I'm building a fortress
>>for my dreams,
>a concrete playground
>>where my heart's patience
>waits safely for you
>>to bring the key.
>
>I'm building a lighthouse
>>from the inside out.
>A spiralled beacon of strength,
>>flashing like a distant star;
>I send this message
>>to illuminate your journey.
>
>I'm building a sand castle
>>one grain at a time.
>As one bead of time
>>slips through my hands
>and the tide rushes in
>>washing it all away.

Dr. Marvin was very intrigued by this poem. "Just what are you building, Eve? Do you even know?"

"This is a symbolic poem, Doc. In the first stanza I'm building self esteem. It's a place where I'm free to be me. Where no one can break my heart."

"What about the keeper of the key?"

"The keeper of the key is just my dream lover."

"And what does your dream lover look like?"

"I don't know."

"Does he look like John?"

"No."

"Does he look like your brother or your father?"

"Fuck you, Doc," I spat, "I think you've got a chronic narrow mind. You just can't grasp the concept that blood is thicker than water. You just can't accept the fact that although lovers come and go, my brother will always be my brother. I think you're jealous and insecure. I think you want me to have nothing to believe in but your fucking gospel of sanity—your fucking flimsy degrees in their fancy picture frames—your fucking Freudian order that rots your root-rutted mind. You're wrong Doctor Deity. You're dead wrong!"

Dr. Marvin's gentle brown eyes barely blinked. He cleared his throat and pointed to the poem in his hand. "So, what is the message you're sending to your dream lover, from the lighthouse in the second stanza?"

I choked back a blood-boiling scream of intolerance and murmured, "He's the tide that finally takes me away."

Dr. Marvin knew that I knew that he knew the essence of my magnetism to certain substandard male species. But I knew that he knew that I knew I must confront this essence myself.

I thought I knew. The poster in my cell reminds me—I DON'T KNOW!

THIRTEEN

Dr. Marvin wanted to know (even though he didn't believe me) how far I could travel out of my body. I told him that I could go anywhere, but that some places were dubious and I was a bit scared of them. He thought that the whole O.B.E. world that I spoke of was an analogy for my emotional terrain.

"What places are you afraid of?" he asked.

"The black holes," I said, "The black holes are the only thing I'm unsure of . . . I mean, I don't know how far they go."

Dr. Marvin thought this was a poetic expression I was using to help myself bridge a gap of understanding. He thought everything had to do with the psyche.

I discovered my access to black holes in space one freezing afternoon in the third grade. I didn't know what black holes were then. I still don't. But I know this:

1) Black holes are omnipresent at the quantum level and the universe is endlessly turning itself inside out through this *Black Magic*.

2) The Sandman travels through the black holes to get from one dimension to the next.

Our whole grammar school was subjected to the mundane task of I.Q. (Irrelevant Quotient) testing. The dead silence pounded me into an altered state of submission. I stared at the dots on my test sheet and began to see a pattern. I filled in the missing dots to the pattern and my eyeballs began rocketing in spasmodic configurations around the pattern into an ever tightening black circle. I was sucked in like a mote of cosmic dust into a vacuum-black hole. It was blind-black. It was white-black. I couldn't breathe. I was paralyzed by some inexplicable G-force. A painless pressure was building between my eyes ready to explode, ready to fuse, ready to invert. But my fear held me back. *I snapped back to solidity like a thunder-crack. I lifted my head from my test paper, and blood was oozing out of my nose.*

I told the school nurse that nosebleeds run in my family. The nurse called Mom at Dino's Diner and told her that I needed a humidifier. Mom borrowed a humidifier from Mrs. Jones and made me stay in my room for two days with a miserable mist blowing in my face. I developed a wicked cough and a blinding fever.

Mom took me to see Dr. Farkis. (The same doctor, who would, years later, refer me to Dr. Marvin for my "dizzy spells.") Dr. Farkis was friendly. He pressed on my glands and my sinuses with soft, spongy fingers and declared, "What you need child, is the special-sick-stopper-formula, and a lollipop." He chuckled like a department store Santa and handed me a red, cellophane wrapped, safety-pop.

"Thank you." I said politely, "Nosebleeds run in my family."

He chuckled like a drunken, department store Santa, handed Mom a prescription, and suggested, "Maybe your daughter should be wearing socks. It is . . . um . . . snowing . . . you know . . . Mrs. White."

Art also runs in my family. My mother was a painter, B.C. (Before Chaos.) She used to paint sensual pictures of seashells and sunsets. She also painted dramatic portraits of bearded shepherds, (which remarkably resembled my father.) And she ended her career by painting a tumultuous crucifixion scene with my father, dripping black blood from the gaping holes in his body and black tears spilling from his eyes as lightning was striking the barbed wire crown on his translucent skull. Dad was mad. He torched the painting in the fireplace. Mom has not painted since that day.

Grandma Black, (Mom's mom) was also an artist. Actually, she was a grammar school music and art teacher. Grandpa Black owned a roller skating rink. They went to Bermuda in 1967 and never returned. Mom says that their plane crashed and they are dead. I say, they have discovered inversion and are probably peaking in the realm of artistic awareness even as I write.

My brother, Robert, is a blues-artist-guitar-wizard-god. He can bend notes from the barely audible vibration of his magic fingers into wailing sounds that alter the transient core of reality. He stretches notes into inversion. His music burns the black right out of the sky.

My blood sister, Jooly Jones, believes as I do, that love is art. She weaves intricate tapestries of crimson castles, misty-eyed unicorns, and stoic dragon slayers. And she weaves herself right into the life of the fabric as a fragile fairy, flitting about with a golden needle trailing her magic thread. Jooly Jones possesses no immunities against the germ cells of romantic delusions.

Some people say you're not really an artist until you're dead. My father is dead. He had a unique niche in the artistic panorama. He built our humble home. He built a hutch for my rabbits that looked like a gingerbread house. He built a manger one Christmas for our plastic, light-up, nativity scene on the front lawn. He built the granite fireplace that he torched Mom's painting in. He built the rocking chair that he died in. My father was a victim of art. Like the canonized boy, St. Innocentius, he no longer had any use for the ostentations of physical reality. Like St. Innocentius, his spirit would not ascend to inversion until he had returned to the earth.

Dr. Marvin said that I found the connections of art in my family because I had looked for them. But I say, all energy sources are connected via the bigger picture, which is the universal sphere of art. The connections are there. It is our perspective which prevents or allows this awareness.

Of the women who share with me this common space, called prison, only a few are aware of our interrelatedness. Only a few are certain that we have been brought together by a higher order than the judicial system. Only a few are willing to lower their resistance to the concept of multiple dimensions. Only a handful of prisoners understand that the keys to the universe of miracles are held within the confines of their minds.

Dr. Marvin used to say that miracles are a case of mistaken coincidences. But I assure you, the lower your immunities are to the awareness of all energies as miracles, the more the universe will openly display its awesome creativity to you.

FOURTEEN

My first real boyfriend, Geoff Sherman, was not a case of mistaken coincidence. He was not tall, dark, bearded, or stupid. He was horny. He was sixteen. He had a lovely Adam's apple. We met in our high school psychology class. We were assigned as partners for an experiment on trust. I blindfolded him and led him around the school campus. He trusted me implicitly. Then he blindfolded me and I got scared. He put his arm around me and said, "Trust me Eve. I won't let you fall. Nothing can happen to you as long as you hold on to me."

I fell morbidly in love with Geoff Sherman. I wanted to have his children. I wanted to make him eggs, sunny-side up, for breakfast every morning. I wanted to grow old and wretched with him.

We rode to school together in his sixty-five, rag-top, Mustang. We went to MacDonalds and had cheeseburger orgies. We drove around town mellowing out on "Pink Floyd" tunes blaring from the mega-watts-per-channel car stereo. We smoked pot and cigarettes. We kissed and fondled each other tenderly. We dreamed big.

Geoff played an electric guitar. He taught me how to play too. We were gonna be Rock-n-Roll stars. We asked my brother, Robert, to leave his band, The M&M's (a.k.a. The Mushroom Mashers) to join us, but he hated Geoff. (Imagine that.) So we recruited a drummer and a bass player and set up to jam at my house.

The problem with jamming at my house was my stepfather. He was a wormy-geek-unpredictable-asshole-alcoholic. His name was Ted. We called him Ted.

Ted was a welder. He was always filthy. Mom married him when I was twelve. They did not fight as much as Mom and Dad had. Mom was tougher than Ted. My dad had taught her some highly effective war strategies. However, Ted liked to fight with me and Robert.

He usually sat in his moss-green, tattered, reclining chair, drinking bourbon and watching TV till he passed out every night. Ted was not very receptive to our musical excursions in the garage. On our third night of practice he got mad and stormed into the garage with a shotgun. His face was purple. Blue veins bulged in his neck and popped through the sparse strands of greasy, gray hair on his shiny head. We stopped playing.

I said, "Hey Ted, we were just about to wrap it up for tonight. Right guys?"

Ted wasn't even looking at me. He pointed the gun at Boomer. Then he pointed the gun at me. "We stopped playing, Ted," I said, "you can go back inside now." Then he kicked a hole in Boomer's bass drum and spun around and fired a shot at me. The shot took a chunk off the corner of my amplifier. "You're fucking crazy!" I screamed. "I'm calling the cops!"

"You go right ahead," he spat as he staggered out of the garage, "and next time I won't miss."

I was scared. Boomer was pissed. Geoff thought I was crazy. "Why won't you call the cops, Eve? The guy's a maniac."

"Because, I won't be living here that much longer anyway."

"What's that got to do with anything? The guy's wacko and he's got a gun."

"It all evens out in the end, Geoff. Ted will pay the price for his actions without any effort on my part."

"Yeah, but in the meantime there's no telling what your cost is."

My cost as Dr. Marvin saw it, was my inability to be honest with myself. He said that I spent my entire life building walls of denial to protect myself from feeling any pain.

But I say, without walls the roof would surely fall in. Walls give structure to the labyrinth of perception. That's all.

Because none of us were academically inclined, Geoff, Jooly, and I dropped out of high school in 1977. We spent the next summer looking for tolerable employment so we could get an apartment together. Jooly got her job at the cookie factory. Geoff and I got jobs at Dolls Incorporated.

We made dolls, painted dolls, dressed dolls and packaged dolls. It was a creepy place to work.

We rented a crummy, two bedroom apartment on the north side of Chicago. It didn't work out too well. Geoff got tall. Geoff got a beard. Geoff got stupid.

Geoff had joined a band without me. I respected his talent and his need to express himself musically, but I resented his not asking me to join the group.

Then, Jooly moved out and got an apartment with her boyfriend-du-jour.

I got lonesome because Geoff's band either practiced or had a gig every night of the week. Geoff had said he didn't want me to come to practice, because I distracted him. I was alone for the first time in my life, and this wasn't what we all had planned.

I told Geoff how lonely I was, and he said, "Why don't you find a friend, or join a band, or something?"

I said, "What about your band?"

He laughed, "Our band is not a hobby, Eve. You're just looking for something to take up time."

Geoff got dark. His band, The Devil's Dogs, were acquiring a following of hell-raising whores and hedonistic drug hounds. Geoff started drinking Wild Turkey and acting like a vulture. He came home with large groups of heathens to raid our cookie jar and to destroy the few scraps of used furniture we had managed to buy.

The Devil's Dogs began getting popular after Geoff was written up in the Chicago Tribune, for assaulting a priest. The priest was standing outside one of their shows, preaching about the evils of rock-n-roll. Geoff picked the priest up by the scruff of his clerical robe and threw him into a trash bin in the alley.

After the great press release, Geoff started wearing a black leather loin cloth on stage and a barbed-wire crown on his head. He also painted black tears running down his cheek. He looked just like the painting my dad had burned in the fireplace. I felt Zoned. I felt haunted. I felt like I was caught in a perpetual circle of torment that had begun at my father's birth.

Although I thought I loved Geoff unconditionally, I couldn't bear watching him turn into a drunken madman.

I ran away.

I ran in a circle.

The Circle

> Walking through the snow
> > I follow footprints going my way.
> Imagine that, I say
> > Someone else has tried to run away.
>
> And I know you will lead me
> > to myself.
> And I know I will find you
> > looking for me.
>
> We make the circle complete,
> > you and me, always out of reach.
> You and me, always free.
> > You and me, always.

Dr. Marvin asked me what I was running away from.
Dr. Marvin asked me who I was looking for.
Dr. Marvin asked me a lot of stupid questions.
Honest.
    I knew deep in the crater of my heart that Adam Sault would understand my ambiguous words. I knew that his life was beginning to revolve around the mystery of my open soul. I knew that he was beginning to make plans for the day when I would expose myself to him. I knew that I was reaching the core of his innermost dreams and that no one before had ever, ever touched him in such awe inspiring places of the mind. I knew, oh yes, I knew, that Adam Sault was aching to touch me, burning to explore me, and waiting in his lonely dreams for a clue, any clue as to answer his questions about me. A clue; a poem that would seize him blindly into love's senseless inversion.
    When I sent Adam Sault the poem, "The Circle," I also sent him a photograph of my feet. (I was wearing purple socks in the photo.) I had no idea at the time that Adam Sault was interested in photography. I was simply staring at my feet that day and decided that they would create a photogenic mystery to keep Adam Sault intrigued. I knew that Adam Sault would see the connection between the poem and

the photo. I knew that he would understand me completely one day.

Dr. Marvin asked me when I would stop running.

"You don't understand, Doc, I'm not really running anywhere. Honest. I think that actually I'm climbing to new heights of artistic awareness. That's all. I think that the illusion of motion is what is confusing you. I think that you're looking only at the pattern of my life and not at the color or texture or mood or values. I think that the pattern you see of my getting involved with the same kind of men over and over is creating an illusion of perpetual motion. I think you're looking at just one piece of the puzzle. I think you need to open your eyes a little wider to take in every angle of my vast picture."

Dr. Marvin asked me if I had any idea just how confused I sounded.

"What do I sound confused about?"

"It sounds to me like you've created a mess of your life and you're trying to attach some sort of artistic achievement to your gross misinterpretation of your pain."

"It sounds to me, Dr. Marvin, like you think my life should be different than it is. It sounds to me like you think I should fit into some kind of neat psychological gallery of your narrow scope . . . but I don't. Do I?"

"If you don't think that your life should be different then why are you coming to see me once a week?"

"I guess I'm just a little confused . . . sometimes."

Dr. Marvin said that admitting that I was confused was one of the first steps towards becoming clear. But I say, the problem with clarity is that it's always subject to weather.

FIFTEEN

After I ran away from the gruesome rock-n-roll affair with Geoff, I moved in with my brother and the M&M's. They had a huge loft space on the west side of the city. Their band was getting tight, like heavy and light. All they needed was a lead vocalist. Imagine that.

My brother, Robert, was not crazy about my vocal abilities but Excellent Ed, Buddy Boy, and Richard were wild about me. They convinced Robert that I had the potential to turn The Mushroom Mashers into, The Magnificent Mushroom Mashers!

Richard, a.k.a. B.D., a.k.a. Big Dick, was the keyboard-songwriting-guru of the band. He was brilliant. He was witty. He was also very tall, dark, bearded, horny and stupid.

We were developing a very natural rapport. He helped me set up my "tent" in the loft. He climbed up the rafters and tied up some ropes and then we strung my pink flowered bed sheets up between them. "That's exactly what this place needed," B.D. declared, "a feminine touch!" Then he peeked inside my tent and said, "You don't have to worry about the other guys creeping in here at night, just me."

Our chemistry was dangerous. Our relationship was budding like a musty basement with mildew. When I got home from the cookie factory every afternoon B.D. was there with exciting ideas for the band. He would make us fried bologna sandwiches for supper, then we'd sit down and write some really deep songs. Our harmonies were growing tight like width and height. We were creating innovative music with astonishingly original lyrics i.e.; "The Shampoo Tune" and "Insomniac Stew."

I was attracted to B.D., that's all. I needed this new musical family more than I needed to have my heart carved open again. So, out of respect for the group's mutually satisfying interactions and our ultimate goal of quality musicianship, I kept my desire for a romantic excursion with B.D. locked within the safe prison of my pulsating heart.

We had practiced every waking moment for three months and Robert finally landed us a gig. We went out to celebrate. B.D. ordered a bottle of champagne and proposed a toast, "To the magic of the Magnificent Mushroom Mashers!"

"Cheers!" We all clinked our glasses in unison.

B.D. poured another round. "And I might add, to Robert for landing us the gig and most of all for bringing his talented little sister to our humble band."

"Yeah!" Clink. Drink.

We talked about what we were going to wear to the gig. We talked about having an empty wheelchair parked in a handicapped zone on the cover of our first album. We drank. We danced. B.D. grabbed my hand and dragged me out on the dance floor for a slow romantic song. He got real, real grindingly close and whispered, "Evie, baby, you are really beautiful."

"Richard, baby," I moaned, "you are really drunk."

"No, I'm serious." He said and started molesting my back with his hairy hands. "You really turn me on."

"I can tell." I said, grinding my hip bone into his brass Marlboro belt buckle. I wanted him right then. Right there on the dance floor. I wanted to wrestle him to the ground and make him shake like a jello mold.

When we sat back down at the table, all sweaty and starry-eyed, Robert asked me to come outside with him for a minute. So I followed him. It was a cool June night. I shivered when we stepped out. "What is it, Bro?" I asked, "It's freezing out here."

"Eve . . . I'm only telling you this because I care about you." His eyes were plastered marbles, the shine had been dissolved by the booze. He looked sad and more like our dead dad as each year passed.

"OK what?" I always tried to hear my brother out.

"Um, I thought you should know before it's too late . . . B.D. has V.D."

"Oh c'mon Robert, gimme a break. What're you telling me that shit for?" I stared at him in disbelief of his inappropriateness.

"I just thought you should know before you fall into bed with him just because you're drunk."

"Yeah, and what makes you think I haven't already?"

"Trust me, Eve. I just don't want to see you get hurt again. B.D.'s got a filthy reputation and he's earned every crumb of it."

"Mind your own goddamn business, Robert. I mean it!"

I stormed back inside. I drank so much champagne that night that Robert and Excellent Ed had to carry me up to the loft. They left B.D. passed out in the car.

The great gig that my busybody brother had arranged for us was a "Battle of the Bands" concert on the Fourth of July, in Grant Park. The prize was a recording session at a local studio. Our first round in the competition was against The Devil's Dogs.

I had told myself before we got to the park that Geoff and The Devil's Dogs didn't stand a chance. And I would simply and completely ignore Geoff. I was much too infatuated with B.D. for the moment to even give Geoff a cool hello. And controlling my emotions would give us the edge over the Dogs. But the universe had other plans in store, the universe was tired of my writing such boring and safe scripts for myself. The universe decided that a Zoning was in order.

The sun was melting and oozing hot pink waves of drama across the western skyline. The crowd was beginning to thicken and Grant Park was looking much like "Insomniac Stew." We were tuned and tight and ready to twirl the park into the inverting force of twilight. Buddy Boy clicked his drumsticks four counts. Excellent Ed popped out a slick lick on his bass. Robert and B.D. fired a funky selection of scales at each other. I screamed out, "AAAAAAHHHHHHH!!!!!" as if the very skin of my soul was stretching, bursting, exploding like an atomic mushroom cloud. We went into the first chorus of "Stew" and as I'm squealing, "Take me bayybee—Rake me down into the sunrise—Oooh yeah!" my sensual, ethereal voice was suddenly inverted into that of a Cuddly Duddly dog. I looked left. I looked right. Everyone was laughing. I kept singing, hoping the sound technician would straighten it out. But it only got worse. Geoff and the Dogs were howling and just having a barking good time. I made faces at Robert to do something but he just shrugged and nodded to keep singing. Halfway through the

"*Shampoo Tune*" I sounded like Cuddly Duddly having a hernia and the crowd started booing and throwing beer cans on the stage.

The Dogs devoured us. The entertainment papers claimed that the M.M.M.'S were, "a substandard attempt at comic relief." And the universe was chortling right along with them.

Dr. Marvin said that the band was my attempt to be important. He said that what went wrong with the gig was that I had experienced an auditory hallucination, which frightened me into tightening my vocal chords.

"Doctor," I said, "The Magic Mushroom Mashers were great. I was great. I didn't have to attempt to be important, I was important. That band never would've gotten out of the loft if I hadn't imposed my insignificance on them."

"Where did they go from there Eve?"

"They didn't go anywhere."

"Why not?" he asked insincerely.

"Because I dropped out of the band."

"Why did you leave the band if you were so wonderful, Eve?"

"Do you ever ask anything besides why, Dr. Marvin?"

"How does it make you feel to be asked why, Eve?"

"It makes me feel guilty, like your accusing me of some wrong doing."

"All right then, what were your reasons for leaving the band?" he asked while drumming his pencil eraser on his note pad steadily.

"I moved out of the loft," I said a bit too poignantly.

"What inspired you to move?"

"There's something strange with your brother," B.D. said to me the day after the fatal gig.

"What do you mean?" I asked.

"I mean after the gig I said to him, 'I can't believe that two speakers blew out at the same time, man. The odds against that are phenomenal.' And he says, 'I told you guys Eve shouldn't sing with us but you wouldn't listen.'"

"Robert is just jealous because he wants to be the star of the show. He'll get over it next time we play and bring down the house."

"Well that's not all, Eve, this morning I was in my tent and I was writing some lyrics for a song, just on paper, ya know. And I was stuck, trying to find a good chorus or a hook and all of a sudden, Robert sticks his head inside my tent and says in his psycho voice, 'In

the garden.' and then he laughs and disappears. And this song I'm writing—I swear, is about Adam and Eve and original sin . . . I mean . . . how could he know that?"

"Oooh, that's really spooky B.D., next stop the Twilight Zone," I chuckled.

"I don't like it," he said. "It's creepy."

When I confronted Robert about "In the Garden," he said, "Oooh, that's really spooky, next stop, the Twilight Zone."

"I don't know why I moved," I parried Dr. Marvin's every attack. "I just wanted a change. That's all."

"What kind of change?"

"A change of direction I guess."

"And where did you go that time, Eve? And where are you going to go next time?"

Dr. Marvin said that I needed to find my niche in life. I didn't know what he meant at the time. I thought he was trying to talk me into a corner, where I would feel safe.

But now I know that a niche is only a transient state of mind where we realize that all destinies are equal, and they always return to the source. That's all.

I had to keep running towards myself. The band had failed and there was no point in my hanging around waiting for my brother to interfere with any more of his bizarre hocus pocus. My brother was like the Sandman, always on the sidelines watching me.

I told Dr. Marvin that I believed the Sandman would somehow guide me to my niche in life. I said, "Perhaps there is a larger purpose for me than you or I can see."

"The Sandman is an extension of your pain, Eve," Dr. Marvin said plainly. "You've got to stop evading the issue of your father and start looking at reality."

"Which reality are we talking about, Doc, yours or mine?"

"There's only one reality, Eve, it's called your life."

"My life is not real the same way as yours is, Dr. Marvin. You just don't see that. Everything in my life disappears before I really get a shot at it. Everything is lost in my peripheral view, and when I turn my head to see it, it vaporizes. The band, my father, Big John, Rodger Badger, the Sandman, they're all different layers of the same invisible cake. That's my reality cake, Dr. Marvin, I have it, but I sure can't eat it."

It's like most of the food in prison.

SIXTEEN

Dr. Marvin often questioned my beliefs. He believed that most belief systems were constructed of insecurities. "Do you believe in God, Eve?"

He asked me this at the time that I was wholeheartedly considering the option of suicidal inversion.

"I don't know what I believe anymore."

"Well why don't you tell me what you used to believe and how that has changed."

"I'm just not sure, Doc. It seems like there's really nothing to believe in. Every time I have believed in something and placed my faith in belief I have been discourteously awakened to a new truth."

"Give me an example of a belief you had that was replaced by a *new* truth."

"Well the first one I remember was when I was about five years old. We were on our way back from a two-week vacation at the cottage in Blue Lake, Michigan, that our family used to rent. I had lost my little toy plastic horse named Pal, and I was crawling all over the station wagon looking for it. Mom said it was probably back at the cottage, but I told her that Pal was crying and running around in the back of the car when we were leaving because he liked it there, and he was sad to leave. I said, I knew he was in the car. So, Mom told me to pray to St. Anthony. She said that St. Anthony hears and answers all prayers for loved ones who are lost. So, pray I did. For the entire ride home I was in silent meditation. I knew that St. Anthony would lead Pal back to me. I believed. I believed with pure unrestricted conviction. And when we got back and unpacked the car there was no Pal."

"How did that make you feel?"

"Well, I asked Mom why St. Anthony didn't bring Pal back to me and she said, 'Sometimes God has other plans, Eve, but don't worry because he hears all our prayers and knows what is best for all.'"

"And how did that make you feel?"

"Well, I started praying to God then. I didn't believe in St. Anthony anymore."

"And did God bring your toy back?"

"No, but she told me that she had made Pal into a real horse and that he was very happy."

"Is God a woman?" Dr. Marvin asked quite seriously.

"Gee, Doc, I really don't know. Do you think if I had a clearer perception of God that my problems would dissolve?"

"I think that you are denying your feelings about God."

"I really don't have any feelings at this time Dr. Marvin. I'm numb. I'm an empty gun."

"Are you a child of God?"

"What God?"

"The God that told you about your toy horse."

"That was a long time ago."

"And what did she sound like? Did she sound like your mother?"

"No."

"Where did you hear her voice? Was it just in your head?"

"Actually, her voice was coming from the heating duct in the bathroom. It was kind of a whispering echo. It was very comforting."

"Did this voice talk to you often, Eve? Or was it a secluded incident?"

Dr. Marvin was frantically writing notes during this session. He really thought he was on the trail to my "delusionary-anxiety disorder."

"Doc," I said, "honestly if the powers that be have something to say to me, I just never know what voices may rise or where the voices will rise from. Haven't you ever heard the universe sending you a message? Haven't you ever really listened?"

Listen . . .

    Two hearts beat
        like wings upon
    a cage of bones.

>   Two hearts impaled
>   in one transient moment.
>   Listen . . .
>   to the voices lost
>   in the rapture
>   of time,
>   gorging on their
>   final overture.
>   Listen . . .
>   to the voices
>   folding over
>   like brittle pages.

Dr. Marvin was quite concerned about this poem. He asked me what the *voices* sounded like.

I felt sorry for Dr. Marvin. Everything seemed so complicated to men with such linear brains. I imagined that Dr. Marvin was the kind of person who avoided supermarkets because the merchandise was not in alphabetical order. I spoke very slowly so that he could understand. "The . . . voi . . . ces . . . sound . . . like . . . lit . . . tle . . . bub . . . bles . . . break . . . ing . . . in . . . to . . . lit . . . tle . . . vi . . . bra . . . tions . . . and . . . ech . . . o . . . ing . . . a . . . round . . . the . . . cos . . . mos . . . hav . . . ent . . . you . . . ev . . . er . . . lis . . . ten . . . ed."

He increased my dosage of V and sent me to the hospital to take a Personality Evaluation Test. Imagine that.

SEVENTEEN

Voluntary manslaughter is a popular crime here. (It's one of the bonding aspects, which has sealed the seams of our interconnectedness in prison.) Baby-Jane and Calamity-Jane are doing time for popular crimes. Baby-Jane and Calamity-Jane are identical strangers. They are the same age and the same size. They have the same face and they were arrested on the same day. Honest.

Baby-Jane Barker was arrested on July 4th, 1985, for the bludgeoning death of her 22-year-old drunken boyfriend, Jimmy Baker. Allegedly, young Jimmy Baker was celebrating Independence Day by throwing firecrackers at innocent passersby on Chicago's Oak Street Beach.

Baby-Jane says, "I told him to cut it out or somebody was gonna get hurt, but he just kept lighting them and laughing. Then he went too far. He threw a firecracker at a little lost puppy and when the poor thing went up to sniff it, it got its nose blown off. I went berserk. I picked up the closest weapon I could find which was a three-pound shard of concrete with a rusty reinforcement cable sticking through it, and I just whacked him as hard as I could in the back of the head. Until he stopped breathing."

Similarly, Calamity-Jane West was riding her palomino, Pal in the Oak Park Independence Day Parade. Pal was twenty years old and had pranced through many parades. Jane was riding tall in her proudest western costume including the genuine pearl-handled Colt revolvers flashing at her sides.

Calamity-Jane says, "Pal was never spooked by loud noises or gun shots. In fact, before I bought him he used to ride in a wild west show. But when that fat kid threw the firecracker, it hit him in the eye. He reared up and I fell off. And my pistol just sort of went off and blew a hole right through the fat kid's skull."

Baby-Jane and Calamity-Jane are playful creatures. They believe that they are destined for something supernaturally heroic when they get out of here. They believe that only God could bring two identical strangers together and so, it is with total respect for this unusual turn of molecular events, that they are regarded by some inmates as messengers of infinite wisdom.

B.J. and C.J. are born-again Christians. They believe in salvation and they have saved a handful of sinners from the ravages of prison lust.

B.J. and C.J. believe that they are open to the truth. They say that prison is part of the Lord's plan. They believe that prison will set them free from their preconceived paths to truth.

But I say, is not belief just another prison?

EIGHTEEN

Six o'clock. Head count. Pup is missing. It's easy to disappear here. They will find her. They always find her. Half dead.

Pup has been resurrected from seven suicide attempts in the last two years. Suicide is not permissible behavior in prison. She will lose *all* of her *privileges*. They will give her medication to make her sleep. Then they will put her in the hole for a week.

Six-fifty-five. Breakfast. Runny grits. Runny powdered eggs. Runny noses. We are cold. Cold as toast. We eat fast. I search for muffins. Muffins are delightful. Muffins are marvelous. Muffins are friendly. Muffins are food for thought. Muffins are fluffy tears of joy. Muffins are warm little breasts. Muffins are genuine. Muffins are peaceful islands in the gray sea of slop. Muffins are golden clouds of enlightenment. Muffins are perfect planets. Muffins are the humble cousin of the cosmic cupcake. Muffins are meaningful mountains. Muffins are unconditional love manifest. Muffins are the exalted, unknowable answer to the unaskable question. That's all.

Seven-thirty. Work. Working in the laundry is a privilege. It is a clean job, but somebody has to do it. Back home I used to hang out at the laundromat. In fact sometimes when I have O.B.E. here I go back to my old laundromat.

The Sandman often appeared to me at my old laundromat. The Sandman is the entity that Dr. Marvin could never believe in. The Sandman is part of the bigger picture.

I am luminous. I am tumbling in the dryer. It is dizzying. There is a comforting hum in the machinery. Patrons are plugged into the yellow plastic chairs like dough. They shift ever so slightly. They fold their faded fabrics with an unseen rhythm. They pat their neat little stacks of underwear affectionately. There is grace and undisputed purity here, and the Sandman comes here too. The Sandman helps make our dreams come true. He helps open the door for those who dare to enter.

Dr. Marvin was very suspicious of the Sandman. He said that the Sandman was a symptom of my "Disorder." He said that I had created the Sandman out of my fear of abandonment. But I say, Dr. Marvin was jealous. That's all.

"What does the Sandman look like, Eve?"

"Well, he's just sort of made up of swirling golden dots. He's just kind of mellifluous."

"And why do you call him the Sandman?"

"Because when I try to touch him he slips through my hands."

"Does this Sandman talk to you?"

"Not exactly."

"What exactly doesn't he say?"

"Well, I'm not certain, but it seems that the voice is a function of the physical body so we can't really talk when we leave the body."

"Then how do you communicate?"

"We sort of just *hang* inside of each other for a few moments and feel the vibrations."

"Eve, I want you to think about what you've just told me and answer me honestly; if the voice is a function of the physical body then what is the vision? How do you explain what you see if you leave your body without your eyes?"

Dr. Marvin was severely rutted in the scientific explanation of perspective only. I tried not to shake up his solidity too much. "Close your eyes for a moment, Doctor Marvin," I suggested.

He closed his eyes and I asked him what he saw.

"I don't see anything, Eve."

"*Don't look with your eyes, Doc. Take a deep breath. Relax. Breathe deeply and slowly. Let your thoughts fade. Imagine yourself in a black room. The entire room is made up of black magnetic tiles. The floor is a spongy black mat. Now sit down. Plug yourself into the mat. There's a vibration you're feeling. It's on the outermost layer of your skin. And the black magnetic force begins peeling away your protective conscious. Your weight is being lifted but you are plugged into the mat. Your thoughts are beginning to swirl through your mind very fast. Too fast for you to think them. The vibration of the* magnetic walls is tugging at the fleeting thoughts, one by one it is absorbing them, it is freeing you. You are totally weightless. As each thought is pulled away, a light is rising inside you. The light is coming from your solar plexus. It is a warm glowing ball. As the light begins to grow you begin to see your luminous self. What do you see, Doctor?"

Dr. Marvin was almost gone. A string of drool dangled from the corner of his mouth. He muttered ever so peacefully, "I . . . see . . . a . . . white . . . a . . . per . . . fect . . . white . . . ball . . . ."

"Now let the light out. Let the ball roll around the room. Is it rolling?"

"Yesss . . . ."

"As the ball rolls it is breaking into little dots. Each dot is an eye. Each eye sees the other eyes. Can you see the eyes, Doctor?"

"I . . . see . . . a . . . zill . . . ion . . . dotsssss . . . ." He trailed off into the abyss.

"Look toward the sound of my voice, Doctor. What do you see?"

"I . . . see . . . a . . . pink . . . string . . . of . . . dots . . . swirl . . . ing, . . . out . . . of . . . a . . . um . . . elec . . . tric . . . cen . . . ter . . . ."

"And where are your eyes. What are you seeing with?"

" . . . I. . . . don't . . . know . . . ."

"But you know you are seeing?"

" . . . Per . . . fect."

"Take a deep breath, Doctor. The magnetic energy in the room is fading and your luminosity is coming back to your center. The room is turning white and your thoughts are rushing back at you. Your thoughts are filling you up with weight. You can feel the black mat again. You can open your eyes."

When Dr. Marvin popped back into his body he yawned. He looked at the notepad in his lap. "Well, how do you explain vision, Eve, if the eyes are part of the physical body?"

"What time is it, Dr. Marvin?"

He looked at his watch very confused. He had left his physical body for thirty-five minutes. "Um, It's already after eight . . . ."

"Imagine that," I chimed. "I'll see you next week."

Dr. Marvin said that I was *severely* confused by my overactive imagination, which was a by-product of my unwillingness to accept reality. He said that reality was not something that I could create.

"Are you sure?" I asked him.

Long silence.

"Do you think that the Sandman is real, Eve?"

Thick silence.

"I don't know."

I cannot know how the Sandman planted that poisoned apple for me to deliver. I cannot know all of the coordinates that have placed me in this artistic dimension. I can only speculate what might be reality from my perspective, but I cannot limit reality to what is knowable.

I can only speculate what might have happened if I had told the judge and jury the truth about the Sandman. I would not have been given a fair trial, and I would have been sent to the loony bin, Randall Perkins said, "In no uncertain terms." But if I admitted to delivering the apple with malice aforethought then I would be committing perjury against myself. I did not know the apple was poisoned. Honest.

NINETEEN

The second day in court Randall Perkins was stammering and shuffling papers. I told him that he should try vitamin V. I was still taking 100 milligrams a day while I was in the temporary holding facility. It was becoming increasingly clear that I was a vitamin V junkie. I was popping in and out of my body like a narcoleptic groundhog. I witnessed bits and pieces of the sordid trial and blinked back out into the bubbly, micro-dot O.B.E. world where nothing is strange.

Tina B-M-O came to court flaunting her vampire smile. She was wearing a sleazy black dress and gobs of gooey, black eye makeup. Randall Perkins was querying her with professional nonchalance.

"Ms. Tolier, can you identify the person whom you claim to have seen at Eden's Gate on the night of June 28th, 1987?"

"Right there!" She pointed a long, black painted fingernail at me.

I was sitting all wrapped up in the tan shawl that Jooly Jones had given me for my last birthday. Randall Perkins had told me to try and look somewhat demure. I was also wearing a pink gingham dress with a matching bow in my hair.

"And were you acquainted with this person prior to seeing her at the bar?" Perkins pecked.

"Well, ya know, we weren't really acquainted, but she was in my drawing class, and I like, saw her around, ya know."

Tina yawned. I wondered if she was about to have O.B.E. Randall Perkins parried her yawns with increasingly boring tactics.

"So you saw Ms. White at Eden's Gate on June 28th, 1987, and what did you see her doing?"

Tina yawned again. "I don't know. I guess she was just sittin' at the bar staring kind of dopey-eyed at her beer. Ya know."

"No, Ms. Tolier, I don't know. Was she or was she not just staring kind of dopey-eyed at her beer?"

"Well, ya know, come to think of it, I guess she was eating an apple and writing something. But I didn't think nothing of it cause she was always a little weird. Ya know?"

"No, I don't know. Will you tell the court why *you* say she was weird?"

"Well, ya know, she just kinda like never talked to nobody. Ya know. And she would do weird things like, she'd like, eat apples in class and go, CRUNCH, CRUNCH, CRUNCH and like really annoy everybody. And, I might add, she drew some really, I mean *really* weird pictures. Ya know?"

Randall Perkins addressed the Judge, "I have no further questions for the witness at this time, Your Honor, but I would like to present some evidence pertinent to the witness's testimony."

"Witness may be seated," the judge sighed.

Randall Perkins's hands were squeaking as he began to assemble an aluminum table easel. "Your Honor," he chirped, "I would like to present as Exhibit A, the completed drawings from Ms. White's drawing class with Adam Sault."

"Objection, Your Honor," the D.A. said, lifting one cool clean finger as if to show the courtroom his manicure. "That is immaterial to the proceedings of this trial."

"Sustained," declared the jibing judge.

"Your Honor," whined Perkins, "I wish to establish the depth of the defendant's character through the sensitive, self-expression of her art."

"Overruled. Mr. Perkins, you may attempt to establish the character of your client."

Perkins picked up my portfolio upside down and the drawings fanned out across the floor like a deck of dusty playing cards. He scraped them up and plopped them down on the table and put one on the easel, sideways. It was the apple composition. A couple of jurors chuckled. Perkins blushed and righted the picture. He extended a telescoping pointer and proceeded to bore the entire courtroom with florid phrases about my art.

"This apple," Perkins proposed, "appears to be an ordinary apple in every aspect, but upon closer examination we can see that the shadow of the apple is shaped like a heart."

Dr. Marvin had noticed the same thing about the apple composition. Dr. Marvin and Randall Perkins, alike, were amazed by their superior ability to detect hidden symbolism. These men were as deep as petri dishes. What they failed to notice were the oblong speckles on the apple that qualified it as a rare Granny-Mac-Blue hybrid apple, which is cross-pollinated in only one tiny orchard located in Blue Lake, Michigan.

Perkins droned on about my use of pointillism and how it takes concerted discipline to develop the kind of patience required to draw in this style. He then added, "However, the most unusual part of this drawing is on the back." He turned it around to face the courtroom. "The comment from Adam Sault, 'A-plus, very sensual!'"

Perkins paused as if he had expected a gasp from the assembly. When it was not forthcoming he turned over the next drawing. "The next drawing was designated in the course outline to be, 'An object partially wrapped in cloth'." He stood back and held his arms out wide.

The object I chose to wrap was a crucifix. I used a tattered linen cloth and left only one corner of the cross showing with Jesus's tiny fingers poking out. I thought this drawing was sad. Dr. Marvin said it was profound. My brother said it was pretentious. But what mattered most was what Adam Sault thought.

Randall Perkins babbled on about my sensitivity and stopped abruptly to flip the picture around. He waved his pointer around like a spastic symphony conductor and said, "The comment on the back suggests that Adam Sault had deviate and unprofessional intentions. It says, 'A-plus! Eve, your talent is amazing. I'm anxious to see what else you can do. A. Sault.'"

"Objection, Your Honor," the D.A. said casually. "Mr. Perkins is suggesting a double entendre, which there is no way of proving. Therefore the comment is irrelevant. I ask that it be stricken from the records."

The judge, the D.A. and Randy-boy went several rounds on this issue. I was getting dizzy and beginning to tremble. I was staring out into a swirling sea of gray faces. Who were these people, I wondered. And then I wondered why I wondered and so on, and I felt myself entering the strange realm of I.B.E. (Inner Body Experience). (I.B.E. is different from O.B.E. in that it exists in the dimensions of inner-space rather than outer-space.) There was a whooshing noise over my head. I looked up and felt my body sinking into my chair. My head bobbed around on my shoulders for a moment and stopped to focus on my feet. My feet were growing green roots and spreading out across the courtroom floor and spiralling up around the table and chair legs. I looked at the jurors, they seemed not to notice this unusual turn of molecular events. Out of my peripheral vision I saw Tina B-M-O lifting a basket up over her head. My roots were beginning to sprout little pink and white flowers, and Randall Perkins was rambling on in some unquotable language with wet consonant sounds. The entire courtroom was curling up with color. Moist tears of laughter were swelling in the jurors eyes. Tina B-M-O started skipping around the room with her basket and handing out apples. She was singing in a screechy little voice, "An apple a day keeps the wormys away! An apple a day and now she's gonna pay!" The judge took an apple and started crunching on it. Perkins was still droning on in wet consonants and he stopped to take an apple and then the jury started crunching, and then the whole courtroom was crunching. The little pink and white flowers on my vines were turning into apples and ripening and falling onto the floor like rubber balls. The crunching courtroom became a deafening buzz and I tried to lift my hands to my ears but they were suddenly clamped to the chair with steel cuffs. The bailiff came in from a back room dragging a seven-foot wooden cross. He dropped it on the floor in front of me. This was it. I was going to be crucified! The jury members all tossed their apple cores on the floor and stood up. The judge rose from his bench like a circus elephant on his hind legs. The crowd cheered as he towered over me and tossed his apple core at my feet and spat, "Guilty!"

Randall Perkins unplugged me from my chair and helped me out to the paddy wagon to return to the holding facility. "Don't worry, Eve," he assured me, "I think that today's testimony really threw them a loop. Tomorrow they'll be certain that you're innocent when we present your poems. Your poems will speak for you, Eve, and then we'll really have the upper hand."

TWENTY

Adam Sault ignored me. I had started mailing the poems to his home address about two weeks before the drawing class had ended. I signed them in red ink, *Severely, Yours.*

I ignored Adam Sault. He was attractive. That's all. He had wavy, chocolate brown hair that curled up at his shirt collar like a gentle splash. He had meaty fingers and smooth, dark, soft little furs brushed finely over his cavalier fists. His ass was round and tight. His legs looked long and strong. (All of them.) His beard was neatly trimmed to highlight his rugged jaw and scenic cheekbones. His nose was almost, but not quite, entirely unremarkable. His nose was cute. Beneath the silky fronds of his moustache were the pale pink, tender petals of his luscious lips. But the eyes of Adam Sault were my undoing. The eyes of Adam Sault did not follow the bouncing ball, they retrieved it—they melted it. The eyes of Adam Sault did not question, they answered. They answered the unaskable question.

Inside Out

  Would you look at me
if I wore my inside out?
  If my true light bolted to the surface
would you close your eyes?
  Would you close your eyes
and listen to my heart pump?
  Would you feel my breath
slicing through the black ice?
  Would you feel the heat
of my grinding skeleton?
  If you saw me melt
would your eyes ignite?

> Would your eyes ignite
> a new fire, a blue fire?
> Would my fervid hunger fuse
> your inside out?

Adam Sault avoided me. He didn't look at me. He didn't talk to me. He was speechless. He wanted me. He wanted to touch me. He wanted to tell me that he wanted to touch me. I was his destiny incarnate. I was the pivot point in his meaningless existence. I was the great karmic resolve he had ached for all his empty lifetimes. I was the *Love Muffin!*

All these immense realizations were unfolding to me as if I had known them all along. Patience, I finally understood. There was no need to rush into Adam Sault's arms like a starved actress. He would see my inside. He would know my voice. Each poem would reveal to him the pure, white fire of my soul. Each word so carefully selected would ring the timeless bells of his crystal spirit. Each breath he breathed would release him from the bondage of physical perspective. He would see through my eyes. We would fuse the distance. Patience would show him the endless path to love and together we would leap into boundless waters of the heart. That's all.

Dr. Marvin wasn't sure what the poem, "Inside Out" was all about. "What message are you trying to communicate, Eve?" He tapped his pen uselessly on his notebook.

"What word don't you understand?"

"What is your *true light*?"

Now I knew Dr. Marvin wasn't faking amnesia about his O.B.E. Nobody ever questions what *true light* is once they have *seen* it. "True light is the pure essence of self, Doc. The free spirit, and all that jazz. How can you not know any of this? Haven't you ever read any poetry besides mine? The spirit is ageless. The poets have been writing about the heart of matter since the beginning of time. The poets let the light out, doctor. They have no walls. No immunities. No fears of the unknowable. Pick up a book sometime, Dr. Marvin—Sexton, Shakespeare, Whitman, Emily Dickinson; the wisdom of the ages—THE VOICE OF DIVINITY MANIFEST!"

Dr. Marvin thought too much. "If poetry is so liberating," he hummed, "then why are you experiencing anxiety?"

"Because I think too much."

"What do you think would help you not to think too much?"

"I'm trying not to think about thinking."

"It sounds like you're trying to deny what you're feeling."

"If that were true, I wouldn't be writing poetry."

"I think you're using the poetry as an escape. I think you're using poetry the way you've used men. I think you want to stay sick, Eve."

It was easy to figure out what Dr. Marvin wanted me to say, "You think I'm sick?" I appeased.

"What do you think?"

"I already told you, I think too much."

"OK, what do you feel?"

"I feel like finding a real doctor."

"That's good, Eve. What kind of doctor are you looking for? Somebody who will put you on even higher doses of medication so you don't have to deal with life at all? You can just float around in a daze. Is that what you're looking for?"

"You're terribly funny, Doctor. You're a real howl. How about a doctor that doesn't accuse me, or a doctor with a little compassion for his fellow mortals?"

"What do you think I'm accusing you of?"

"I think . . . you're incapable of understanding the spirit world."

"Eve, I think it's time you stepped into the real world."

"Can't they be the same, Doc?" I asked.

He just stared at me. Unblinkingly.

Dr. Marvin wasn't very highly evolved. I pondered the possibility that all tall, dark, bearded men might have some kind of genetic quirk which limited their intellectual capacity. Then I pondered the possibility that I was somehow projecting these qualities on to these species, and that in fact I was the one with the grave limitations.

Adam Sault would be different. I had convinced myself that this genetic link—this physical allure, would be broken by virtue of my words. Adam Sault would see the beauty of my soul within my words and he would find the same root in his own soul and be forever transformed.

Dr. Marvin said that the root of my problem was that I needed to make peace with my father, and that until the past is resolved no one can have peace of mind. But I say, the past is always resolved. It is the present moment only in which I can be peaceful.

TWENTY-ONE

"My dad doesn't owe me anything," I told Dr. Marvin after he suggested that I felt abandoned. "I am responsible for my own misery."

"A parent's responsibility is to take care of his children. Did your father take care of you?"

"Perhaps my father had a higher responsibility to take care of himself."

"How does that make you feel?"

"I accept it. That's all. I don't need to know the destiny of anyone but myself."

"Do you think that if your father had taken responsibility for his family, his destiny might have been more favorable?"

Robert and I were sitting quietly on the carpet, watching The Dick Van Dyke Show. We were amused. Rob Petri was having a dream about growing lettuce on his head. Dad was sitting in his rocking chair behind us sucking down his fifth scotch and water. (I counted because I had made them.) It was our birthday. Robert turned eight and I turned seven. Mom came out of the kitchen singing Happy Birthday. She carried a plate with devil's food cupcakes with two little candles burning. "Make a wish," she said.

I looked at my dad. My dad was sad. I wished he would die. Mom went back in the kitchen and brought out two pretty packages, one with a pink bow, one with a blue bow. "Your father made these for you," Mom said without a smile and went back into the kitchen.

We unwrapped them carefully. They were little wooden treasure chests. They had little brass locks with keys. We unlocked them. They were empty. Dad laughed and shoved a cupcake in his mouth. "Thanks, Dad," Robert and I said politely. Dad laughed again and started gasping for breath. The cupcake was stuck in his throat. He was making gurgling noises and grasping for his drink. He knocked his drink off the table. Robert ran to get Mom from the kitchen.

Dad's eyeballs were popping out towards me. He was trying to say something like "H . . . E . . . L . . . ." I watched him turn from red to violet to indigo. Mom came out and put her arms around Robert and me and held us tight. Dad finally collapsed in a heap, like a great circus tent. Mom tossed a white sheet over Dad and called an ambulance. We stared mechanically at the TV till the ambulance arrived.

Rob and Laura Petri had, comically and charmingly, come to terms with reality. They always did.

Dr. Marvin asked me if I felt guilty about my birthday wish. "Why would I feel guilty, Doc?" I asked.

"Did you feel somewhat responsible for your father's death?"

"Of course I felt *somewhat* responsible. It was my wish. But what does guilt have to do with birthday wishes?"

"You assume responsibility for your father's death and you feel no remorse?"

"I don't claim complete responsibility. There are many other mysterious powers that must coordinate for one wish to come true."

"What mysterious powers do you think were responsible then?"

"One, Robert, also had a birthday wish. Two, the molecular components of the cupcake had to be just right to lodge itself into an impenetrable morphogenesis in his throat. And three, Dad had to laugh at exactly that moment."

"Do you know what your brother's birthday wish was?"

"He wished that I should have whatever I wished for."

Dr. Marvin said that I was creating the story of cosmic synchronicity to relieve myself from guilt. But I say, guilt is a device used to promote moral conscience with the underlying belief that humans are naturally evil and will turn to destruction without a thought. Being human means that we are subject to inhumane thoughts and actions. If this paradox did not exist we would not be human. Hence, the ultimate act of moral conscience is taking responsibility for being human with all its paradoxes and implications. Being human gives us the choice to feel guilt or to forgive. And forgiveness of everyone, including oneself, is the responsibility that most conscious humans seem unable to assume.

"Don't you think that your father's actions might have been different if he had felt guilty about the way he treated his family?" Dr. Marvin persisted.

"I don't think that my father had the components necessary for evaluating his own consciousness. Meaning, he was possessed by another form of consciousness, something perhaps more compelling than the reality that you and I are able to comprehend."

Dr. Marvin shook his head. "That's all intellectually enticing, Eve, but how does it make you feel? And how did it feel when you were just a child wishing that your father would die? And how did it feel when he did die? How can you not feel guilty?"

"I don't know," I said, realizing for one flash of a second that maybe Dr. Marvin was right. Maybe I felt so guilty about killing my father that I would spend the rest of my life seeking his forgiveness. That was absurd, of course, because in the next flash of a second it occurred to me that this guilt was a seed planted by Dr. Marvin. It had nothing to do with how I really felt.

I just needed some more time to discern my purpose. Some more time and some more Valium.

TWENTY-TWO

Ma says that guilt was invented by psychiatrists and religious zealots. She hisses vehemently, "It'sss much eathier to condemn than to condone. People are lathy. And your esstheemed Dr. Marvin is a tree ssthloth looking for a plathe to hang hith indolent labelsth."

Pokey says to Ma, "I'm not lazy. I'm just not in hurry to get to the great burial ground."

Pokey, a.k.a. Pochahontas, a.k.a. Julia White Deer, is my Indian Spirit Guide. Pokey is the mistress of patience. We have spiritual rap-sessions together where she guides me to the calm waters where the White Deer of the North Woods will one day empower me with the gift of transformation.

Transformation by Pokey's explanation is a magical ability to transform the physical presence of a human into that of an animal such as a bird or a cat.

Pokey is large. She is not related to Pochahontas. She is half Sioux Indian and half Eskimo. Ma named her Pochahontas because she said we needed an Indian princess to look up to. We call her Pokey because she moves in slow motion. She maneuvers herself passively through space as if she doesn't want to miss a single sensation.

Pokey is doing time for murder one. She decapitated her Supreme Nemesis; her husband. Pokey says that she had married him to make him her ally. "He was a very powerful Medicine Man when I met him," she says with a fierce tone. "Nicoa White Deer had many gifts. He forgot that I was also a gift. He lost much of his natural powers when he began drinking the sour mash whiskey. He tried to steal my power. He tried to break my spirit."

Pokey tells me that people are virtually unaware of the forces that guide them through the universe. She says that we are always in contact with dual forces, our allies' and our nemesis'.

When I asked her why she whacked off her husband's head with a machete she said, "There are only two ways to end conflict with the Supreme Nemesis; one is to make it your ally and the other is to kill it before it kills you."

Pokey writes poetry too. Pup is very jealous of Pokey being my Spirit Guide. Pokey says that Pup is her nemesis and my ally. Pup likes to start fights with Pokey. She likes to run away with her tail between her legs and come crying to me. "I'm gonna kill her, Muffin. I swear one day she's gonna be sorry she ever went to prison." Pup is my ally because I am learning to have patience with her childish behavior. Patience means never having to say, "LET ME OUT OF HERE!" Patience is a state of wonder.

Ten forty-five. I was wrong when I said they would find Pup half-dead. She was having a meeting with the chaplain who visits us. She has earned the privilege of meeting with him solely on the basis of her self-destructive tendencies. The chaplain looks like a squirrel monkey. He has tearful, black eyes and a small, round, shaved head with little pink ears. He told the warden that it would be emotionally beneficial for Pup to be free to talk to him at will.

When Pup strolls in to the laundry room she is wearing a spiritual smile. Pokey points out that I was wrong, Pup is not half dead. I love to be wrong. Being right offers no enlightenment. I cannot learn that which I already know.

Eleven-thirty. Lunch. Fighting is not permissible behavior in prison. The guards stroke their billies affectionately. Pup throws a bowl of pea soup in Pokey's face. Pup is clobbered by the time the guards even see there's a commotion.

Noon. Back in the laundry. St. Birdy is singing . . . "Don't-be-cruel-ooooh . . .Don't be crooool . . . Doeoeoen't beeee sooo . . . ."

Pokey tells me that she is sorry for hitting Pup. "I feel like a hypocrite telling you that patience is your virtue when I have no patience with that bitch."

"I trust your judgement, Pokey. Your relationship with your nemesis is your business."

"I'm just having a tough time making an ally of her."

"I think that she wants your attention and that's why she picks fights with you. She really wants to be your ally but she has animal defenses against her inner nature. She needs to make allies with the beasts within before she can begin to take a step outside herself."

Dr. Marvin wanted to know what beasts I kept locked inside my head. He thought that the treasure box my father had made for me contained some sort of unspeakable monster from my past. "There's nothing in the box," I told him. "Except some rocks and sand."

"What are the rocks for?"

I wasn't sure what he meant, "Well, different rocks are for different things, Doc," I said.

"What do you do with the rocks, Eve?" he clarified.

"I found the rocks by my dad's grave the day he was buried. About a year later I found that the rocks were turning into sand."

"If you have resolved the past as you claim, Eve, then why do you keep the rocks?"

"Because I think they're what brought the Sandman to life."

"Why do you need the Sandman, Eve?"

"I think we need each other . . . I think that's how it works."

Dr. Marvin would not, could not believe that the Sandman was real. In his vast educational training, the subject of paranormal manifestations was considered unworthy of scientific pursuit. Henceforth, he could only see my problem as an intellectual-emotional based delusion.

"I think you have a lot of secrets, Eve. And I think you want to share your secrets but you just don't trust anyone."

"If I tell you something, Dr. Marvin, and you betray my trust, who wins?"

"Have you ever played to win, Eve?"

"Do you always answer a question with another question?"

"How does that make you feel?"

That question. That fucking question always reduced me. "It makes me feel like I'm talking to myself."

"And how does that feel?"

"It feels like I'm going in a circle. I get dizzy when I listen to myself for too long, Doc. The dialogue is ceaseless. There's a jackhammer pounding on my heart. There's a Mardi Gras churning in my belly. *A CLOCKWORK ORANGE* is the feature film at my mental drive-in. The Beatles' White Album echoes backwards through my brain. The only repose I have ever found is O.B.E., and I'm beginning to think that a permanent departure might be the path of least resistance."

"Are you contemplating suicide?" he asked seriously.

"I don't know ... I mean ... no ... Not suicide as you understand it, just a change of direction if you will."

"What direction would that be?"

Dr. Marvin was reaching for his prescription pad. I reached out and tugged on his fine, gray suit sleeve. "No!" I cried, "I don't want to sleep anymore! Waaah ... Waaah ... Ug ... gg" I turned on the tears.

"What do you want, then? Do you want to talk?"

"Ug ... g ... g ... I ... just ... want ... g ... g ...." I held my breath and then let go a lonesome howl, "HHHHEEELLLPPP! WWAAAHHH!"

He increased my dosage of V and sent me for more psychological tests.

Dr. Marvin said that until people know what they want out of life they will experience constant anxiety and feelings of uselessness. But I say, you've got to want what you have before you can have what you want. And all that you have is your *being*.

TWENTY-THREE

After I had been in therapy for about nine months, Jooly Jones confronted me at work. "What's going on, Eve?" she asked. "Why are you so down?"

I just shrugged my shoulders and said, "I don't know."

"Let's go out after work today," she said. "I want to talk to you."

We went to a nearby shopping mall.

"How's the art class going?" she asked sincerely.

"It's OK. I have a crush on the teacher."

"Do I know him?"

"You might. He goes up to Eden's Gate sometimes."

"What's his name?"

"Adam Sault."

"Not the tall, dark, bearded, horny and stupid Adam Sault that hangs all over Tina-B-M-O?"

"I've never seen them together."

"Oh sure, they were the talk of the town for awhile. Tina told his wife about their affair and his wife valued her honesty so much that she gave her a job at her frame shop and let her move into her house."

"Imagine that."

"He's a worm, Eve. You don't need any more worms. It's time for you to move into a higher realm than mere physical attraction."

I wanted to listen to Jooly. Jooly was a genius. She saw facets of the artistic panorama that only those with no immunities could see. Dr. Marvin was right, I had barriers.

Jooly bought me a peppermint ice cream cone and we sat by the waterfall in the center of the mall. "Tell me what's really wrong, Eve. I want to help. I love you. We're blood sisters. We're The Women's Anti-Gravity Association. We can't let each other down when the gravity is low."

I looked at the waterfall. All that water, I thought, just goes in a big circle. It gets sucked into the black pump and falls again and again. "Jooly, when does it end?"

"When does what end?"

"When does the perpetual reclamation come to an end? When do we stop reincarnating? When do we reach the golden apple?"

"As far as I know it never ends. It just has new beginnings."

"Dr. Marvin thinks I'm crazy, Jooly. Do you think so too?"

"You're a little weird, but you're not crazy. You're just at a crossroad of introspection right now. Now is the time for you to ponder your ineffable name."

I pondered my ineffable name.

I watched the waterfall.

I saw the waterfall.

I heard the waterfall.

I fell.

Jooly jumped in and grabbed me before I went over. My peppermint ice cream cone didn't have time to scream. The water turned pink below. The shoppers gaped.

Jooly put her shawl around my shoulders and steered me out to her car. "What kind of medication does the doctor have you on?"

"It's just Valium. Nothing exotic."

"Does he realize how despondent you're becoming?"

"Of course. He says I'm making progress. He says that healing is painful."

"Do you trust him, Eve?"

"I don't know if trust is part of my genetic makeup. I'm not sure what trust is."

Dr. Marvin said it was imperative to my recovery that I trusted him.

"How do you process trust Doc? How do you know who's gonna fuck you up until they do it?" I had told him about the waterfall at the mall and what I had said to Jooly about trust.

"Do you trust Jooly?"

"What do you mean by trust?"

"Do you feel that Jooly would ever do anything to hurt you?"

"Jooly would only hurt me if it were in my best interest."

"Do you trust your brother?"

"Robert has his own set of rules and values."

"Do you trust him?"

"Robert has a tendency to interfere, but his intentions are for my own good."

"Do you trust him?"

Dr. Marvin could be so unidirectional sometimes. Sometimes it took all my strength not to strangle him with his own wimpy, yellow silk tie. "I love my brother, Doctor. Why is that such a BIG FUCKING PROBLEM FOR YOU?"

"Don't be upset. I want to know what your capacity is for trust because I think you may be helped by hypnotherapy."

"You want to brainwash me?"

"I want to help you to redirect your psychic energies so that you can focus on the real issues."

The real issues Dr. Marvin was talking about were the tangibles. The foul relationships. The dismal career situation. Dr. Marvin said that I was hiding my head in the lofty clouds of spiritual issues and that until I straightened out my earthly issues I would never understand the complexities of life. But I say, life is not complicated, people are.

TWENTY-FOUR

Blue Beard was complicated. Blue Beard was a biker. He was my boyfriend after B.D. (Who never really was my boyfriend.) Jooly and I were on our way home from work one day when I pointed to the shiny row of motorcycles in front of T.J.'s TAP, and said, "Let's go in there, Jools. Let's do something really crazy. Let's go get our butts tattooed!"

"Are you kidding? Those people are savages. What would you want to go in there for?"

"Oh, don't be so righteous. We haven't done anything wacky in a long time. I say a Zoning is in order!"

Jooly drove around the block twice. I counted twenty-seven Harley-Davidson motorcycles backed up to the curb, leaning like an army of fat tulips into the sunset. Jooly parked her car around the corner so that they wouldn't know what we were driving. I told her to act casual, "Act like you belong and nobody will notice us."

The ripe aroma of beer, tobacco, sweat, and leather wafted over us as we opened the door. I froze. I had never seen so many tall, dark, bearded, horny and stupid looking men all in one place. Jooly pushed me, "Oh, you really look casual with your mouth hanging open," she said as she steered us toward the bar. There were two vacant stools between two brutish looking dudes. We sat down.

Blue Beard had apparently been attacked by a mad tattooer. His skin was crawling with cartoons: eagles, skulls, roses, dragons, and a heart with the name "LEFTY" in it. (And that was just on his right arm.) I was trying not to stare. He waved his hand in front of my face. "Haven't you ever seen a tat before, babe?" he asked invitingly.

I looked up and saw this raw, primitive, angel's face. "Um ... actually ... I've never seen so many," I smiled.

"You babes wanna brew?" he grinned sweetly.

I nudged Jooly who had been trying to get the bartender's attention. "Hey, babe" I said, real seedy, "you wanna brew?"

She looked at Blue Beard and then at me. She looked at the brute sitting next to her. She looked at the jukebox, which was blasting "Born to be Wild." (Honest) She looked at the black leather vests with the gaudy back patches that read, "Heaven's Devils." She looked back at me and mouthed "No."

I looked at Blue Beard's friendly-furry face and said, "A couple brews would be swell!"

He opened his mouth and bellowed, "BEER HERE!"

A stringy-haired blonde creature behind the bar filled three pitchers and put one in front of each of us. "How 'bout a toast to tits!" B.B. declared. Jooly and I raised our pitchers up to his, clanked them and said, "To tits!"

Blue Beard bottomed out his pitcher in about thirty seconds. Jooly in about two minutes. Me, in about two hours.

While Jooly was off shooting pool with Catman, (the beast that was sitting next to her) I asked Blue Beard how he got his name.

"Everybody gets a name once they're in the club."

Blue Beard was incapable of giving a straight answer. I asked him if it hurt to get a tattoo. He replied, "Pain has nothing to do with tats."

He asked me if I was a virgin. I said, "What kind of a question is that?"

He said, "You look like a virgin."

"What does a virgin look like?"

"A virgin ain't got no rug burn on her elbows."

B.B. asked me if I wanted a shot of J.D. I said, "What is it?"

He laughed. I was really amusing to him. He ordered me a shot and said, "Drink this. It'll make your nipples hard."

I did. It did.

He picked me up then, carried me outside, and put me down on the back seat of his "scoot." He stepped back and declared, "Perfect!"

My head was loose. I wondered if Jooly's head was loose too. "Igggotta go," I slurred, "nicze talkin' t' you." I got off the bike and staggered inside.

I went to the bathroom and turned on the cold water. I gargled my face till I could feel it again. The sink was filthy and smelled like urine. I barfed. I felt better. Blue Beard walked in as I was swishing my mouth with the cold water and chomping on a peppermint LifeSaver I had found in my purse. "You OK?" He asked affectionately.

I shook my head vigorously from side to side. "Where's Jooly?"

"Yer buddy took off with the Catman about two hours ago."

He took me by the hand then and led me back out to his bike. I leaned against the seat. He looked at me with a look that could melt the moon and said, "I wanna take you for a ride, baby." He leaned over and cupped my face with his greasy hands. The great cave of his mouth parted and his meaty tongue speared through my minty, drooling lips. He slid one hand under my knee and lifted my leg so I was straddling the leather saddle. He stroked his fingers ever so lightly on the inseams of my jeans and then trailed up, up, up to trace every curve and seam on the pockets of my t-shirt. I wanted to ride, indeed!

He lifted me off the bike so that he could kick start it. It was a 1962 Dual Glide 1200 CC MONSTER. He named her Norma Jean. He was in love with her. She was cherry red and her chrome sparkled like icy-spiked jewels. Blue Beard balanced the weight of his long, lean frame onto the kicker. He leaned forward, grabbed the handlebars, raised his ass up, and with one smooth jerk, Norma Jean was rumbling like a jalopy.

I swung my leg over the back and slid up close to smell his leather. There was a feverish glow to the fat July moon. We sputtered through town and headed for Lake Shore Drive. Norma Jean heaved out onto the drive with a fat, bellowing, THROB! . . . THROB! . . . THROB! My ears popped. We throbbed along the lake for about fifteen minutes before she conked out. B.B. said she needed to cool down. He pulled an Indian rug out of the saddle bag and spread it out on the rocks. I wanted to pass out; B.B. did not. I got rugburn on my elbows and my ass. Imagine that.

Jooly and I joined the Heaven's Devils. They called me Snow White and Jooly was called, J.J. We were *Mamas*. We were property of B.B. and Catman. It was mostly, but not quite, an entirely annoying experience.

I loved riding Norma Jean as much as B.B. did. The awesome throb of that machine between my legs was like a perpetually-regenerating-teeth-clenching-electrically-exploding-multiple-orgasm. (That's all.)

The club went on poker runs to different bars, collecting cards to play the final hand back at T.J's TAP. The club went on runs to Wisconsin and South Dakota to party. The biggest disadvantage to riding with the club was that when the bikes stopped, (or broke down, which was often) we had to get off and have conversations with our Ol' Men.

It was a long summer. My ass was sore. Blue Beard was a bore. I told him that I didn't want to see him anymore. I tried the F-word, "Let's just be FRIENDS," I said.

Suddenly, Blue Beard shows his true colors. He tells me that nobody ever dumps B.B. He says it's time for me to get a tat, "Property of B.B." I tell him I already have a tattoo, Jooly and I got matching butterflies on our butts a month ago. It hurts. A lot. He doesn't care. Tats have nothing to do with pain, says he. I don't want any more, says I. He calls me a disrespectful little bitch. I spit in his face. He breaks my arm.

A week later Blue Beard was inverted. It was a "freak accident," the police said. No vehicles involved. No mechanical failure. He just laid Norma Jean down in the middle of the highway. The paramedics poured bleach on the stained street where they scraped up his scattered tattoos.

I went to the funeral with Jooly. B.B. was laid out in a crisp black suit. His head looked slightly dented and crooked, but other than that he looked as placid as my dead dad had looked.

I knelt in front of the casket searching the sunken eye sockets for movement. He'd had such invadingly-wild eyes, like the cracked gray marbles that had popped out at me from my dad's drunken skull as he choked on the cupcake.

I reached over and laid a white rose by his cheek. There was still not a flutter under his skin. I pressed my hand on top of his, which were clean, and folded comically out of character for him. I felt the silence of his missing soul seeping into my flesh, and vaporizing like alcohol. "Sorry, buddy," I whispered.

Silence . . . . Like my dad.
Silence . . . . Like Rodger Badger.
Silence . . . . Like the voice of the Sandman.

Dr. Marvin said that I went into T.J.'s to try to lose myself, and that I was still looking for a man to replace my father. Dr. Marvin said that I would do anything to feel accepted and loved.

I said, "Try me, Doc."

"Do you see what you're doing?"

"I'm Zoning you."

"No, Eve. You're trying manipulate me so that you don't have to look at the truth."

"Is it working?"

"It's counterproductive to your recovery."

"What's the truth that I'm avoiding, Doc? Is it so wrong for me to look for love? Is it wrong for me to believe that love will set me free?"

"So you do believe in something after all. What do you believe love will set you free from?"

Dr. Marvin got a hard-on every time he thought he was right. I put my hand over my crotch and said, "I believe love will set me free from desire."

Dr. Marvin said that love was the object of my desire, and that I would never know what love is until I loved myself. But I say, love makes no distinctions.

He said that I had wandered so far out into fantasyland that fiction had become preferable truth. But I say, fiction is more powerful than truth because fiction is timeless and boundless. Fiction is eternal. Truth is limited to today. Truth is in a constant state of inversion. Today's facts are tomorrow's jokes. Fiction is multidimensional and therefore possesses no immunities. And so I ask you, is not fiction the essence of discovery? I implore you, is not discovery the essence of consciousness?

TWENTY-FIVE

Lefty has a tattoo on her bicep. "Property of B.B."
Lefty is doing time for burglary. She's a repeat offender. She's not a good burglar. She has two left hands. Honest. She says it is her fate to be a burglar because she can't get a decent job on account of her "left handicap."
I asked Lefty about her tattoo and she said, "B.B.'s my Ol'Man."
"What does B.B. stand for?"
"Blue Beard. The club calls him Blue Beard because he was accused of murdering his wife. He allegedly had told her never to come to the bar. Then, she showed up one day and he was hanging all over some Mama. There was a scene at the bar, and then she mysteriously disappeared. The cops couldn't find a body, so nothin' happened. But the club decided that he killed her anyway, and named him after the legend. He also had a blue beard tattooed on his face for his initiation into the club.
"We're gonna get hitched when I get outta here," she added.
"When are you up?"
"About another two years. I already done two."
"Aren't you afraid he might kill you?"
"He didn't kill his wife. B.B. wouldn't hurt anybody. He's a marshmallow."
"Does he visit you here?"
"No, in fact I ain't heard from him since my trial but I'll find him when I get out."
"Does he have your name tattooed on him?"
"Course he does. My Ol'Man, he's got a million tats."

It is not my responsibility to inform Lefty of B.B.'s inversion. The universe will gladly provide information to those who specifically request it. (In fact, maybe Lefty will discover B.B.'s inversion through this book being donated to the prison library.)

There are no coincidences, and yet nothing is predestined. Dr. Marvin said that I found so many meaningful connections to my experiences only because I wanted to believe that I had a purpose. He said that I would embrace anyone or anything rather than face the truth. But I say, there are truths that exist whether I embrace them or not.

When Dr. Marvin sent me to take the psychological evaluation tests, I thought they were going to hook me up to a machine. Instead they gave me a book with about a zillion questions in it and a true-false answer sheet. It was boring. I found the pattern within the dots and spiralled right out of my body. I went to the laundromat. The Sandman was there. Sparkling. Luminous. I tried to touch him—I always tried to touch him, but he always slipped through my hands. I wondered if he had a body. I tried to follow him as he shot straight up out of the laundromat and sailed out over the city toward Lake Michigan. He had a tail like a comet and I rode on his tail as he dove towards the lighthouse near Navy Pier. He hovered there. I circled around him. Then he disappeared. Poof!

When I sailed back to the hospital, it took me awhile to find my body. It had been moved. (I hate when that happens.) My body was strapped down to a bed with an oxygen mask taped over the face and an I.V. stuck in the arm. It didn't look much like my body the way I had left it. I ripped the mask off and sat up coughing. A nurse came in and slapped me on the back. "Where am I?" I groaned.

"You passed out, Ms. White. The doctor will be right in to see you."

The doctor came in with a clipboard. "Hi, I'm Dr. Gland," he stuck a chubby hand out to me. "How are you feeling?"

I shook his paw. "I feel fine. Would you please remove this foreign object from my vein?"

"Sure I'll do that in a minute, I just want to make sure everything's where it's supposed to be." He pushed around on my belly. "Does this hurt?"

"No."

"What's the last thing you remember?"

"You asking me, 'What's the last thing you remember?'"

He chuckled like a late-night talk-show host, "Ho! Ho! Ho! What do you remember before that?"

We went back to, "Does this hurt?" to, "Please remove this foreign object from my vein." Which he finally did. Then I went back to how I was trying to find my body, and how I hate when that happens.

"Does this sort of thing happen often?"

"No. Just when I'm really bored."

"Does your regular doctor know about this?"

"Yes. Can I go now?"

"Let me call your doctor first." He looked at my chart. "Dr. Marvin, right?"

I nodded. He left and I decided that I better not wait for him to return. After all, this was a psychiatric hospital, he might even be a patient.

When I saw Dr. Marvin later that week for my regular appointment, he said that he was worried about me. I told him that worry, in my experience, had only produced anxiety. "That's my job, not yours," I said. He wanted to know what happened to me during the test.

"I had O.B.E., Doc, why don't you understand that? Did you ever read the questions on that test? Why don't they just come right out and ask me what my anal fantasies are? My subconscious is an open book. What are you looking for? Why don't you just ask me?"

"The test you were taking is designed to detect psychosis and borderline personality dysfunction."

"Boredom-line is more like it. So, did I pass?"

"I want you to take another test."

"I ain't going back to that hospital."

"No, we can do this test right here. It's called the ink blot test. You've probably heard of it before."

Dr. Marvin took out a stack of Rorschach cards and handed one to me. He picked up his legal pad and said, "I want you to tell me everything you see in these pictures, whether you think it's significant or not."

"Everything?"

"Everything."

"Well . . ." I turned the card around, upside down, every-which-way. "Where's the top?"

"It doesn't matter. Whichever way you see an image."

"Are we going strictly for the symbolic image or do you *really* want to know what I see?"

Dr. Marvin would not let me see him scream. "What do you see?"

"Right here . . ." I pointed to a pink splash, "this is a story, Doc. Oh, this is a fairy tale. The pink splash is the forbidden fruit. See how all the other colors revolve around it. And this smear over here is the serpent, the worm, the irresistible evil. These dots are the holes in the ground where the life comes from and where it returns to. This blob in the middle represents the androgynous Adam and Eve before they've tasted the fruit." I handed the card back to Dr. Marvin, who was scribbling away on his legal pad.

"Was that what you wanted?" I asked.

"That was fine." He handed me the next card.

"I think this test is much more revealing than that other one," I said. "Don't you agree?"

I carried on with the next card much the same as the first. Really, they didn't look like anything to me. I got no special vibes or queer reactions out of any of them. Dr. Marvin said that I did fine. I asked him what a normal person's response to the cards would be. He said everyone responds differently.

I was irreverent to Dr. Marvin. It seemed an appropriate defense at the time. He was trying to help me the only way he knew how, with vitamin V and confrontation therapy. I was responding the only way I knew how, by hiding even deeper into the comforting folds of my intellectual blanket.

I had a place for everything in my mind. I had a place for everything except the Sandman. The Sandman could not be wrapped up neatly in my brilliant blanket. The Sandman is beyond fiction. The Sandman is beyond imagination. The Sandman is unknowable.

TWENTY-SIX

In prison, we have a sort of art-therapy session once a week. Madame X is a volunteer art instructor. She brings paints, paper, ink and colored pencils on Sunday afternoons. Madame X used to be a prisoner here. She likes my drawings of lighthouses because she says it stands for hope. (Dr. Marvin would say it is a phallic symbol.)

Many of the drawings and paintings here look like Rorschach tests. The world just has no idea what kind of talent they have locked up in prisons and institutions. I ask you, how is an artist to discover her potential when she is confined to a cage, whether it be a societal dungeon or an academic reformatory? I implore you, is not the most profound art that which is entirely uninhibited?

Four o'clock. Game time. We play poker for cigarettes or money. (Or muffins.) We play rummy. We play chess. We play ping-pong when there are ping-pong balls. Weather permitting, we play volleyball in the yard. The yard is surrounded by guards. Volleyball is a painful game. Two prisoners have died on the volleyball court. Several others have been transferred to other correctional facilities after having a lively game with the gals. Volleyball is a game with transient rules. Volleyball is the only way to have fun while getting your teeth fixed.

Five o'clock. Head count.

Six o'clock. Dinner. Gray meat. I can't eat. It's wretched. I gag. Pokey gives me a Hershey bar. I give her a kiss. Kissing is not acceptable behavior in prison. Kissing is punishable by demerit of *privileges*. And if you have no privileges to be taken away then you will be sent to the hole.

Six forty-five. Showers.

Seven o'clock. TV, or school if you have earned the privilege. I went to school last month. One class a week. I received a certificate which licenses me to wash hair when I get out of prison. Beware!

Dr. Marvin was trying to get me interested in a career. "Have you thought about taking a computer class?" he asked.

"I'm not really interested in working in that sort of environment," I said. "I think I'd prefer a nice cushy job like yours."

"I went to school for twelve years to get my degrees. Does that sound pretty cushy to you?"

"Anything sounds better than baking cookies, Doc. I swear I think I'd rather starve sometimes than go to that oven and get toasted all day."

"What about a secretarial position? If you went to night school you could conceivably get enough credits to be out of the factory in less than a year."

Dr. Marvin offered me every conventional opportunity known to woman. "I want to do something different, Doc. Somehow I just feel that my destiny is much greater than the safe occupations you envision. What about the people with vision? Why can't I be somebody who makes a difference? Somebody who makes changes to help the little people of the world."

"Because you have to start with yourself. You are one of the little people of the world who needs help. I think you need to take a step towards a career. What about nursing?"

"What about letting me decide what I want?"

"Making decisions is not taking action."

"I'm taking an art class aren't I?"

"Yes and I think it's wonderful but you've got to take some more action towards your future or you'll remain locked in the perpetual chain of dissatisfaction."

Action. I pondered this concept. I really was letting life happen to me. I was taking no action towards resolving the conflict within my heart. Action. I liked the sound of it. I said it to myself as I sent each poem off to Adam Sault. Action!

TWENTY-SEVEN

It was easy to figure out what Dr. Marvin thought was a bad idea. He thought poetry and art were therapeutic tools only. I challenged him, "So you don't think I have enough talent to make it as an artist?"

"You're very talented. I just wish you wouldn't limit yourself. I think you could be successful at a lot of things."

"Art is limitless, Dr. Marvin."

"Isn't an artist's income limited, though?"

"What does my income have to do with art?"

"You've got to be realistic, Eve," he said almost pitifully. "You've got to look at the facts. And the facts are that very few artists are able to support themselves by art alone."

"I'm sure that's true, Dr. Marvin, but what about the ones who are truly great?"

"Eve, I don't want to discourage you completely, but there are hundreds, if not thousands, of truly great artists who are working in gas stations and factories all over the world. And it's not that they aren't great, it's that there's a limit to the market. The world only needs so much art."

"Do you really believe that?" I prodded him.

"Unfortunately, Eve, it doesn't matter whether I believe that the world does or doesn't have enough art. The fact is, there are limits today to how much art the world is willing to support."

"Limits are made to be broken like rules," I said confidently. "Limits are merely a matter of perspective. There are rules to perspective, Doc. You can't break the rules unless you know what they are."

I handed Dr. Marvin a copy of a thesis I had started writing upon my recent discovery of artistic awareness. The thesis, I later discovered, had to be backed by exhaustive academic research, and hence, my artistic intentions were thwarted by the invasion of literary qualifications.

Creativity and the Cosmos
A thesis on the network of artistic energies:
by Eve White

Definition-Perspective; n. 1. Various techniques used to represent three-dimensional objects esp. onto two-dimensional surfaces. 2. The interrelational aspects of subjects to each other and to a whole. 3. Point of view.

The rules of perspective:
    A) Everything three-dimensional has a vanishing point.
    B) The vanishing point is an illusion.
    C) Light comes from within as well as from without.
    D) Light is subject to gravitational as well as time warp activity, which alters perspective from every relational point.
    E) Perspective is a transient relationship between the universe and the artist.
    F) $E = mc^2$

Dr. Marvin thought this was clever. "So, Eve, you're saying that if I know that everything three-dimensional has a vanishing point, then I can break that rule."

"Rules aren't broken unless they are understood."

"So how do you break the illusion of the horizon?"

"There is no such thing as a horizon. We only think that we see a line across a lake. There is no line. The water and the sky are interdependent. If there were no sky, there could be no water. Like us, Dr. Marvin—if there were no coordinates, we would not know where you end or where I begin. Perspective is merely a name we use to give us an identity, a point of view, if you will."

There is a fine art called compromising. I had to compromise discussing my artistic theories at certain times lest I leave Dr. Marvin lost in the cosmos. I reached the point on the proverbial horizon and shifted the perspective to something simple that Dr. Marvin could help me understand, like why I was hyperventilating.

I continued in the silence of my paper world to search my heart for the truth. Adam Sault would appreciate my artistic revelations. Adam Sault would understand my message of love, and hear the song of my soul. The game of love would finally reveal its rules. The poetry of life would begin to live. The illusions which led me to the promise of love would be dissolved by the clear, perfect touch of truth.

The truth I did not understand then. I did not perceive that the truth was flexible by virtue of interdimensional perspective. I didn't understand my own theories. I didn't understand the messages that were coming through me. I was locked in the dark dimensions of my own creation. The prison I had built around my heart saw only one key—love.

Dr. Marvin told me that a BIG part of my anxiety disorder was due to my perspective. He said that love is a feeling perceived by two people, and that I had perceived infatuation as love. But I ask you, is not love beyond the dimension of feeling? I implore you, is not love an energy without limitations?

Dr. Marvin asked me if I loved the Sandman.

"I guess so," I said, "I mean, I love knowing that he *is*."

"What do you mean, that he *is*?"

"I mean, I feel graced by his presence. I feel that no real harm can come to me as long as he exists."

"What do you mean that he exists?" Dr. Marvin was getting stuck again.

"I thought you wanted to know about my feelings for the Sandman," I redirected.

"I want *you* to know what your feelings are regarding the existence of something that only you believe in."

"You keep getting stuck on that 'existence' issue, Doc. Why don't you tell me what the difference is between what I believe exists and what you want to hear."

"What I want to hear, Eve, is that you realize that you've pretended this 'Sandman thing' into a god. I want to hear you say that you have pretended long enough."

Pretending

My sister is a unicorn junkie
they trot and gallop
all over her clothes
her apartment
her jewelry.

My lover is a stranger
the ultimate danger
for a lonely heart
for his alluring eyes
may be only an illusion.

My mind
is the gate to magic
where I dance with abandon
to the wind's song
where the unicorns stampede
and where lovers really love.

Dr. Marvin asked me who the lover was in "Pretending."
He asked me why I was pretending.
"How many times do I have to tell you, he's just a symbol of love. I'm just pretending that he exists so that I have a love to strive for."
"And what does that symbol resemble? Your father, perhaps?"
"No, Doc, it doesn't resemble my father. It symbolizes purity, honesty, and humility."
"Does that symbol resemble masculinity?"
"I don't know."
"Does the symbol of the tall, dark, bearded men you are attracted to resemble your father, and your brother, and your desire to be taken care of by a strong man?"
"It symbolizes . . . all men . . . all men in one . . . I know it sounds really corny, but to me the ultimate symbol is that of Jesus Christ. All the pictures I've ever seen of Jesus he had a beard. He looked like such a nice man. He looked loving and compassionate."
"Isn't that what your father looked like, too?"

"Technically, yes, but . . . it's deeper than that, Doc. My father used to preach to me and Robert about sin and hell, and all kinds of hocus pocus. But as I've told you, my father was not exactly Christ-like. And I don't know that I can even begin to understand the implications of "God" or "The Messiah", if you will; but there is a mysterious connection that I feel when I'm in the presence of biblical-type men. There's a haunting loneliness in those eyes that I long to love."

"You want Jesus to be your lover?"

"I want a lover that won't judge me."

"You want a fairy tale?"

"I thought I just said, I WANT A LOVER THAT WON'T JUDGE ME."

"What do you fear being judged about?"

"I want boundless love, I don't want love that's restricted to the physical world. I want a lover that loves my soul and not just my flesh. I want a lover that reads the pages of my life story without judging the book cover. I want a lover who embraces my divine spirit and doesn't care whether or not I make a hundred-thousand dollars a year, or whether I have a big tits, or whether I wear socks to bed . . . or whether . . . I . . . have . . . syndactylism."

Dr. Marvin raised an eyebrow curiously at me. "What do you mean by syndactylism?" he asked.

I walked over to his bookshelf and pulled out his obese medical dictionary. I put the heavy book in his lap. "It's spelled s-y-n," I said.

Dr. Marvin flipped through to it quickly.

Dr. Marvin chuckled.

Dr. Marvin rarely chuckled.

"What is the symbolism behind syndactylism, or webbed feet as it is defined here?" he stopped chuckling.

"It's not symbolic of anything. It's a fact."

"You have webbed feet?" he asked cautiously.

"Webbed feet run in my family."

"You're serious?"

"Honest." I took my right shoe and sock off, and fanned my long, white, froggy toes wide. "My father told Robert and me, that his ancestors were great Atlantians and that because of this special trait, we would have unique powers."

Dr. Marvin didn't look shocked or appalled. He scrawled something on his legal pad. He looked at me sympathetically and said, "If it bothers you that much, why don't you have it surgically removed?"

"That's not the point, Doc. It doesn't bother me at all. In fact I think it's a rather interesting phenomenon. I think my feet are just the way they're supposed to be. But everybody doesn't think like I do. Some people think I'm a freak."

"I don't think you're a freak. Maybe you're just projecting your insecurities onto other people. Who has ever called you a freak?"

It was 1973, and Jooly Jones was once again giving me her rap about karmic inversion and how rude people would be reincarnated into earthworms. She quoted a passage from Genesis; 3:14 "The Lord God said to the serpent, ' . . . upon your belly you shall go and dust shall you eat all the days of your life.'" "What more proof do you want?" Jooly asked me.

"But Jooly" I cried, "he called me a freak." I was blubbering and pounding my fists into her pillow.

"Evie, he's just a boy. He's only fifteen. He doesn't know anything about love. He's ruled by hormones."

"Well I'm only thirteen so what do I know about love?"

I had thought I was in love with Ralph Barnes. He had dark curly hair and asked me if I had an extra cigarette all the time. I knew he was falling in love with me every time I saw him hanging out in front of the drug store, waiting to ask me for a cigarette. I knew he was really waiting for me to mature. So on July 5th, 1973, I seduced him. I bought him a whole pack of cigarettes. He took me by the hand and dragged me behind the drug store and began kissing me with adolescent abandon. He tried to grab my breast and I panicked and pulled away. He asked what was wrong and I just looked around at the dark alley. "Oh . . ." he said, "I know a place where we can be alone." He dragged me by the hand again down the street to his garage which he locked once we were inside. He turned on a black light. There were fluorescent posters on the walls and a mattress on the floor with a Spiderman sleeping bag covering it. He pulled his glowing purple t-shirt over his head and tugged his jeans off. He stood there in his electric purple jockey shorts with his boyish boner popping straight out. I snickered. He sat down on the mattress and pulled me on top of him. I let him wrestle with me for my clothes. I stopped breathing as he poked his little penis inside me and collapsed. He slid off of me like a fried egg and turned on an overhead light. I just lay there wondering whether or not we "did it." He lit a cigarette and plopped back down on the mattress taking a deep, mature drag. "That was your first time wasn't it?" he asked.

"Yeah, I guess," I replied.

He slid down to the end of the bed and started putting his socks on. He saw my feet. "WHAT THE FUCK?" he yelped, jumping off the bed like a toad.

I curled my toes up tight and bellowed "THEY'RE MY FEET ASSHOLE! HAVEN'T YOU EVER SEEN FEET BEFORE?"

"God, that's really freaky looking." He took a deep, furious drag off his cigarette. "Can't you have them fixed or something?"

"THERE'S NOTHING WRONG WITH THEM!" I cried.

He tossed my clothes on the bed and said that I had to leave cause his mom would be home soon. I was crying. He said he was sorry. He said that if he were me he'd keep his socks on in the future.

I slapped his face. He never asked me for another cigarette.

Jooly said that his karma was so bad that not only would he be reincarnated as an earthworm but in this lifetime he would suffer the ultimate male chagrin: when he crashed into middle age his hair would fall out, and he'd get a pot belly.

Dr. Marvin asked me how it had made me feel to be rejected that way. I told him it hurt him more than it did me.

"How is that?"

"Well, when the karmic law catches up with him he'll suffer ten-fold the pain that I felt."

"And that gives you comfort?"

"Comfort is not what I seek."

"You seek to relieve yourself from pain and so you adopt a universal law which gives you peace of mind. I'd say that gives you comfort."

Dr. Marvin would rather have me agree with him than to accept the fact that If I were right about karmic law, then eventually even he might be an earthworm.

The further I delved into my relationships, the more I began to see how significant they all had been. Each boyfriend, though they all appeared to be clones, had prepared me for the next in line. This was an evolution, an artistic awakening. Each portrait would help to set up the scene for the next rendezvous. All to lead me to Adam Sault, and then to prison—the pivot-point of resolve.

TWENTY-EIGHT

Jack was my boyfriend after Blue Beard. Jack was a jerk. Jack thought he was nimble. Jack was attractive. That's all.

We met at Jooly Jones's annual Halloween party. Jack was dressed as the ghost of Elvis Presley. He had a white, rhinestone fringe suit on and white makeup on his face. He was lip syncing "You Ain't Nothin But A Hound Dog" as the record was playing. He sauntered over by me. He curled his lip up and sneered, "That's sure a purdy dress, Ma'am, let me guess . . . Cinderella?"

I snickered. "Positively wrong. Guess again."

"Um . . . Goldilocks?"

"Ugh!" I gasped and waved my fan in front of my face.

"OK . . . Miss America!" He chuckled.

"Really, you should be ashamed." I turned my nose up.

"Well I apologize, Ma'am," he bent down on one knee and half sang, "and I'm beggin' you don't be cruel cause I just wanna be your teddy bear."

I twittered, "Tee hee . . . Very well then." I held out my silk-gloved hand, "RRRRoxane." I let the name roll down my arm and ring into his face.

He lowered his head and turned my hand over, ever so gently, and kissed the inside of my wrist. I got shivers.

Then Cyrano de Bergerac came bounding over. "Is this jester pestering you, M'Lady?" he stared down his long nose at the *Elvis suit*.

I twittered, "Don't be rude, cousin. This is Elvis, he's a very famous Southern Gentleman."

Elvis stuck an eager hand out.

Cyrano snorted, "Another *Christian?* I presume." He bowed slightly. "Excuse me for intruding." He swooshed away.

Elvis nodded at me, "That your boyfriend?"

"No. That's my brother, Robert. He has a serious case of overactingitis."

"Is it contagious?"

"No. My name's really Eve."

"That's good to know, but I really am the ghost of Elvis," he laughed heartily and swayed his hips.

I turned my head and began fanning my face.

"I'm Jack," he chuckled nervously. "Would you like to dance?"

"I would be delighted," I said. He put his hand on my bare shoulder and led me towards the center of the room. It was dark there. Several couples were pressed against each other. Johnnie Mathis was crooning loudly. He pulled me close and we shuffled in a small circle.

"So what is your costume supposed to be?" he broke the silence.

"My brother is Cyrano de Bergerac, and I'm his cousin, Roxane." I looked for recognition in his ghostly eyes, but there was none.

"Never heard of 'em."

"They're characters from a play that Robert and I were in back in high school."

He was unimpressed.

"Robert and I dress up together every year for Halloween. It's sort of a tradition. My mother started it when we were little. We were Raggedy Ann and Andy one year, and a devil and angel the next. Last year we came here as Pierrot and Columbine."

Jack looked baffled.

"It's just a tradition," I offered. "That's all."

Jack worked at a custom door shop. He was a door designer. He was almost smart. Jack said that doors were invented to keep people out and locks were invented to keep people in. But I say, doors and locks are merely psychological obstacles.

Jack had shaved off his beard for the Halloween party. He said, "Who ever heard of Elvis with a beard?"

Jack had juicy lips. We kissed a lot. We went out for pizza and beer a lot. Jack was not very enigmatic. He was a good bowler and a creative lover; without getting graphic, I'll just say Jack made a generous contribution to kinkiness. Imagine that.

Jack and I went on a fishing trip to Blue Lake, Michigan. I had told him that we used to go there in the summer when we were kids and that it was very clean and peaceful.

The universe knew I would be on that trip. The universe knew when to zone me. The universe knows just how to synchronize events in such a way that causes me to consider the possibility that confusion is the greatest illusion of all.

I woke up at dawn. Jack was snoring like a locomotive. I tiptoed outside of our little cabin in my pink bikini underwear and pulled one of Jack's white t-shirts over my head. I grabbed a can of Pepsi from the cooler and lit a cigarette. I rubbed my eyes open.

The wilderness of Blue Lake was oozing crystal dew from every pore. A shallow layer of velvet mist simmered upon the lake. "Awe!" I said aloud, "So this is where the clouds sleep."

I turned on the garden hose to flood the worm bed so they would surface. Then I tottered out onto the slippery pier to check on the survival rate in the minnow bucket. I heard the hum of a small trolling motor. I looked out over the great soup of nature. The head of a black labrador retriever was floating just above the mist, bobbing ever so gently; headed my way. A silver bass boat drifted into the hazy picture beneath the dog and a buffalo man wearing a red Budweiser cap was guiding the motor. He steered the boat towards our dock, cut the motor and coasted silently to the edge of the pier. There were two small bushels of apples in the middle of the boat and some fishing gear.

The buffalo man had a scraggly black beard that rested like moss upon his puffed belly. His hair was tied back in a ponytail that hung just above the visible butt crack of his wide low slung jeans. He tipped his Budweiser cap at me. "Howdy Ma'am! Beautiful mornin'!"

The mirrored sunglasses, the missing front tooth, the chubby-chipmunk-cheeks, the tattered flannel shirt, none of this could fool me; I would know the real Elvis Presley anywhere. I stood there with my mouth hanging open.

He chuckled, "Cat got yer tongue?"

"... Um ... Er ... Um ... No ... I ...."

"M'name's Bud Winters. Folks call me Bud Weiser though," he smiled like a lopsided jack-o-lantern. "I'm the fella you rented yer cabin from."

"... O ... ," I was Zoned.

"I live on the other side of the lake with m'dog, Frog." Frog wagged his tail, jumped out of the boat and galloped off into the woods. "I call him Frog cause he's got webbed feet. You should see him swim."

I looked down at my bare feet. Exposed again! (Jack was one of the few lovers who was not appalled by my feet. Jack thought my feet were funny. Rodger Badger thought they were beautiful.) Elvis looked down at my feet and kind of cocked his head to one side. He smiled and his upper lip curled just like the old pictures, except that the missing front tooth made him look somewhat devious and demented.

"We just thought we'd be neighborly and bring y'all some apples from our little orchard." He lifted the bushels onto the pier and said, "We got my rare hybrid apples here for eatin' and some bitters for bakin'."

He chuckled a little and said, "You OK, Ma'am?"

". . . I . . . um . . . I'm sorry." I shook the shock off. "My name's Eve . . . Um . . . it's nice to meet you . . . Bud." I reached my hand out.

When he shook my hand, I felt shivers. All over. I realized I was standing in my underwear talking to Elvis Presley. I was Zoned. "Umm . . . I was just gonna make some coffee . . . Bud, would you like some?"

"Sure would. That'd be swell." He lumbered out of the boat as only a buffalo could.

I tugged my t-shirt down and said, "I'll be right back."

I bolted up to the cabin. Jack was still thundering down the tracks of slumber. I jumped into a pair of shorts. I filled the kettle with water and set it on the camp stove outside. "It'll be just a few minutes!" I yelled to Elvis as I walked casually toward the picnic table where he had now planted his buffalo body.

Elvis was shaking JUJUBES out of a box into his mouth. He held it out to me, "Want some?" he asked.

"Um, thanks," I said and held out my hand. He shook a few into my hand. I picked out a red one and said, "Red's my favorite. When I was a kid I thought I could feel the colors that I ate." I paused, biting into the redness of the JUJUBE, "Red feels the saddest."

"Isn't it beautiful here?" he asked.

I gazed around, "It's perfect here," I said. "How long have you lived here, Bud?"

"Well I came up here from Memphis 'bout nine years ago."

I cleverly calculated this to be August of 1977, which was when Elvis had allegedly died of a drug overdose. "Why'd you leave Memphis?" I queried.

"Aw, it's a long story. I just couldn't keep up the facade anymore."

"I think I know what you mean," I said, popping an orange JUJUBE into my mouth and feeling a little brighter.

"People will buy anything that comes in a pretty package," he said. "They don't even care if it's empty." He poured the rest of the JUJUBES in his mouth and studied the box carefully, and then handed it to me.

I examined the box. It was indeed empty.

"Why'd you take that box, Ma'am?"

". . . Um . . . I don't know."

"You took the box," he said, "because you don't care. It looks like it has substance, so you want it. Am I right?"

"Um . . . this is really deep," I said. "But I think I know what you mean."

"People want illusions. People can't see without their eyes. They can't look beyond the package and see what's really inside." He gazed out over the misty lake. I assumed he was seeing without his eyes.

"I'll go get some coffee, Bud." I traipsed up to the cabin and carried back two steaming styrofoam cups.

He had put the bushels of apples up on the picnic table and was now holding an apple in each hand. He held them out towards me. "Which apple do you think is sweeter, Ma'am?"

"I don't know," I said. "I guess the redder one."

"What if I told you the spotted one was sweeter?"

"You're the expert, not me." I smiled.

"If you're the one who's going to eat the apple—" he paused and looked at me pensively, "then you're the expert."

"I see," I said, while thinking, Elvis has really drifted far off into the cosmic sea. He looks like a buffalo, and he thinks his name is Bud Winters. He floats out of the mist in a bass boat and he's addicted to JUJUBES. He lives with a syndactylous dog named Frog, and Elvis is trying to share with me some divine wisdom in eating apples. Somehow I knew he was saying something significant to my subconscious that would become clear to me when I needed to understand it.

"Don't you get lonely out here?" I asked.

"The only time I've been lonely, Ma'am, was when I didn't want to be with myself. Like when I was in Memphis. I was surrounded by people. Everybody wanted to be with me, but me. I was so lonely I could die."

He gulped his coffee down and wiped his beard off with his arm. "Well, thanks for the coffee, Ma'am. I've got some chores to do, so I'll be pushing on now."

"Hey, anytime . . . Bud . . . Um, thanks for the apples."

"Those spotted apples Ma'am, I call them "Granny-Mac-Blue. They're my own special hybrid and this is the only orchard where you can get 'em." He tottered into the boat as only a buffalo could. Then he gave a little whistle through his missing front tooth, and Frog came leaping out of the woods and took his position at the stern. He tipped his Budweiser cap at me and said, "Enjoy your life, Ma'am."

With one smooth tug on the cable, the motor started. He waved. Elvis Presley and Frog disappeared into the mist.

I studied the two apples. They appeared quite ordinary except one had tiny oblong spots. I turned them in my hands. I weighed them. I smelled them. I felt their divine energies. I wasn't sure what this meant, but for the first time in my life I saw what apples really looked like. They each had unique personalities. Each had seeds of distinctive wisdom. Each had their own special purpose for coming into my life. I knew how Eve must have felt in the Garden of Eden. How could she not take a bite? The apples seemed to ooze a spiritual power that I could not deny. I took a deep bite from each one of the apples.

They tasted the same. Sour. Imagine that.

TWENTY-NINE

Dr. Marvin asked me how I felt about Jack dumping me to remarry his third ex-wife who had received a two million dollar settlement in the divorce from her fourth ex-husband.

"I don't know, Doc. I guess I felt used. As Robert had told me, Jack was only using me for his deviate sexual excursions."

"Did you enjoy sex with him?"

"More than I did fishing."

"Did you enjoy sex with him, Eve?"

"Is that really any of your business, Doc?"

"It's my business if he hurt you."

"He broke my heart, Doc, not my arm."

Dr. Marvin wanted to talk about my sexual experiences. I did not want to share them with him. I asked him if nothing was sacred to him. He said that I had very deep rooted sexual complexes and that I needed to examine what they were if I wanted to feel better about myself.

"Dr. Marvin," I said, "do you have any idea how archaic your Freudian approach to analysis is?"

"What approach do you feel would be more appropriate?"

"I don't know, Doc. All I know is that I've been coming to see you once a week for over nine months, and we just keep rehashing the same boring details of my past love affairs. And all this rehashing seems to be doing is focusing on my pain."

"What would you like to focus on?"

Silence.

I wanted to focus on my new artistic romance with Adam Sault. I wanted to share with Dr. Marvin the joy I was feeling inside. I wanted Dr. Marvin to know that he really was helping me to open my eyes and my heart to the innermost workings of my unlimited mind.

But I knew that Dr. Marvin was limited. He was not an artist nor could he comprehend the naked truth of art, the wisdom of the poets, or the mystical gifts of the universe.

I wanted to focus on this new reality I was entering. I wanted to tell Dr. Marvin how I was writing poems every day and sending them anonymously to Adam Sault. I wanted to tell him that poetry was the missing element in all my other relationships, and that I had discovered how to give of myself, of my heart, and that this was the true essence of life.

"I had a strange dream last night," I said, instead.

Dr. Marvin nodded and wrote something on his legal pad.

"I dreamt that I was being crucified. You were there, and Jooly was there and my brother, too. The three of you were telling the crowd not to throw the rotten apples at me. Then Elvis Presley appeared and started singing, 'Don't Be Cruel'."

Dr. Marvin tapped his pencil on his legal pad. "What does this dream mean to you, Eve?" he asked seriously.

"I don't know, Doc. I think it's a premonition of some sort. I think it means that my parents imposed a negative image of Jesus on me, and that I will be redeemed when Elvis rises again."

Dr. Marvin really enjoyed hearing my dreams. This was safe. We spent the next two months analyzing my dreams. Dr. Marvin was proud of his insight to symbolism. The more ridiculous the dream, the more it meant to him.

He got really excited when I told him that I had a dream about he and I fucking on the cookie factory floor. He said that I was making progress by identifying my transference. He also said that this dream was really about my father and that I wanted to reunite with him.

"I think maybe you should see a shrink, Doc." I quipped, "You seem to have a really twisted fascination with incest."

"What do you think your dreaming about me means?"

"I think my dreaming about you means that I find you physically attractive. That's all. I haven't been laid in six months, and everything I look at is beginning to resemble penises to me—that pencil you're holding, your fingers, your nose, the legs on your chair—YOUR HEAD! Everything I touch feels sexual, Doc. Do you think maybe I should break my vow of celibacy just so I can concentrate on my mental recovery?"

Dr. Marvin never squirmed. I could have jumped up, ripped my clothes off, and mounted him, and he would have just continued to take notes. Dr. Marvin was a dedicated professional, unlike Adam Sault who had, unbeknownst to me, been building up his karmic portfolio in a less refined manner. But who was I to judge?

THIRTY

Randall Perkins called Robert to the stand. "How long have you known the defendant, Eve White?"

Robert snickered, "Twenty-nine years."

"She is your sister?"

"Since she was born," Robert stated.

"Has your sister ever displayed any violent tendencies?"

"No. Eve's harmless."

"No further questions."

Perkins sat down and gave me a thumbs up sign. Robert scratched his beard as the D.A. approached the bench. The D.A. had an edge, and he was determined to slaughter me. He pointed at Robert with a dagger-like finger and hissed, "Where were you on the night of June 28, 1987?"

Robert flinched. "At work."

"At Eden's Gate, which is two blocks from the apartment where the deceased lived—is that correct?" The D.A. spun on his heel.

"Where the deceased *lived?*" Robert asked sarcastically.

The D.A. smiled happily at his own expense and recovered instantly with, "Did you know Adam Sault?"

"Not personally."

"But you knew who he was?"

"He came into the bar once in awhile, that's all."

"You knew that your sister was in his art class?"

"Yes. So what?"

The D.A. spat, "You knew that your sister was sending anonymous poetry to Adam Sault!"

"How would I know that?"

"Your sister was living with you, correct?"

"Yes."

"You knew that your sister was emotionally disturbed, did you not?"

Perkins objected. The judge overruled.

"I knew she was depressed. That's all."

"You knew your sister was taking medication, did you not?"

"Yes."

"And yet you served her liquor on the night of the murder."

Perkins objected. The judge overruled.

"Yes, I served her beer."

"If you knew she was taking medication, then why did you serve her alcohol?"

"She only had a few." Robert's lips were tightening.

"Didn't you think that alcohol would ease the pain she was feeling from being rejected by Adam Sault?"

"I didn't know anything about Mr. Sault."

"You mean your sister lived with you, and yet you knew nothing of her private life?"

"That's right."

"What time did your sister leave Eden's Gate?"

"She left around two a.m."

"And what time did you leave?"

"I closed the bar up at about three-fifteen." Robert was starting to squirm.

"And you went directly home?"

Robert curled his upper lip. "Yeah, I went straight home."

"What time did you arrive home?"

"Three-thirty," he answered mechanically.

"And your innocent little sister was sleeping like a lamb?"

I looked at Perkins. He nodded.

The D.A. addressed the jury. He told them that the poisoned apple was ingested by Adam Sault between two-thirty and three-thirty a.m. He called other witnesses to the stand who testified to having seen me leave the bar at two a.m. with a basket of apples.

Randall Perkins nodded a lot. Perkins had some oblique tactics up his sweaty sleeves. He called the owner of the fruit stand to testify on my behalf. The little old lady who pushed the fruit cart in our neighborhood said that, indeed, I bought apples from her all the time. Randy-boy was really on a roll. "Your Honor, at this time," he tightened his tie, "I would like to present as Exhibit B, the alleged poems which were sent anonymously to Adam Sault."

"These poems," he went on, "are representative of the defendant's sincerity and innocence. I would like for the members of the jury to review them very carefully before they reach any decisions."

Everyone rose. The jury disappeared. My poems went with them. Now everyone would know the secrets of my soul. My paper dream would be publicly probed. My heart would be reduced to analytical pulp. Perkins nodded and gave me a thumbs-up sign.

THIRTY-ONE

The judge was on the edge of his bench during my testimony of the one and only night I spent with Adam Sault. The jurors were wriggling like worms in a hot bucket. Dr. Marvin looked sad.

I was up at Eden's Gate. It was June 21st, 1987, my twenty-seventh birthday—a year after Big John had tossed me out on my butt. I was not exactly celebrating my independence, but I didn't want to stay home either.

Adam Sault stalked into the smokey room like a hungry panther. My focus was magnetically fused to his inner presence. I had never before been able to look directly at him. This unusual turn of molecular events meant something.

He appeared in front of me like a ghost and asked if he could buy me a beer. I just stared at him. Something was smacking the inside of my brain.

It hadn't actually ever occurred to me that I would ever speak on a personal level to Adam Sault. Even though I had sent him two-hundred and seventeen poems, a photograph of my feet, a pair of purple socks, and several humorous greeting cards; it never occurred to me that I had nothing to say to him. I didn't really have any intentions other than discovering my own artistic potential by inventing an imaginary romance. This was a work of art I was creating, not a trashy romance novel. I didn't really want to expose myself to him. I didn't want him to know who I was. I thought Adam Sault was attractive. That's all.

Eden's Gate was loud that night. Mizz Martha and the Martyrs were wailing in agony over love's lost cause. When I realized that Adam Sault was sitting next to me and asking me something, I began to sweat and shake. I feared that I was having an I.B.E. I looked straight into his eyes for a response. He repeated, "Can I buy you a beer?"

I looked at Robert who was behind the bar cutting lemons with a rancid smile smeared across his face. I looked back at Adam. Adam . . . Adam . . . Adam. I tried to locate the word in my mental data base, but my great computer had shut down. I blurted out, "WHAT?"

He leaned close to my ear and bellowed, "Can I buy you a beer?"

Beer . . . Beer . . . Beer? Hello . . . Hello . . . Respond please. "YES!" I shouted.

The band had stretched their final note of the evening out into a perfect harmony which ended with my "YES!" Adam applauded. The smokey crowd was mellowed now, lulled into the wee hours by the blues. It was raining all over the world—inside and out. Adam Sault was wearing a gray leather jacket which was damp from the rain. The musky aroma made me dizzy. I inhaled deeply through my nose and sighed.

Adam Sault waved at Robert. Robert nodded and poured two mugs of golden wisdom. Adam Sault nudged my elbow, "Are you old enough to drink?" he laughed.

I laughed. "Yeah, I'm real old," I said dumbly.

Where were these words coming from? Hello . . . Hello . . . Operator? You are sitting next to the impeccably gorgeous, bearded, mystery man of your dreams. He is buying you a beer. Hello . . . ? He is smelling of wet leather . . . GRRRR! Say something intelligent!

Adam Sault parted his lips to speak. His mouth glistened like a sticky cherry lollipop. "Don't I know you?" He tilted his head to look beneath my Budweiser cap and into my eyes.

" . . . Um . . . Sort of. I was in your drawing class about a year ago."

"Oh, yeah, I remember you. Please forgive me, though; I'm terrible with names. I remember your drawings, though, very sincere, very deep."

"Eve White," I said, and stuck out my sweaty hand.

"Eve! What an interesting coincidence; my name is Adam," he laughed. His dark eyes sparkled at me. "You here by yourself?" He looked around.

"Um . . ." I looked at Robert who had put our beers in front of us, and was standing there grinning. "Yeah, I'm alone. I live right down the street with my brother, who is standing right in front of you. Say hello, Robert."

Robert said, "Three bucks, pal. We've already met."

Adam chuckled, "I didn't know you had such a cute sister. How come you never brought her around before?"

He flipped a five dollar bill on the bar, which Robert scooped up and spun around to put in the cash register. He spun back around, plopped two dollars in front of Adam, said "Thanks, pal," and disappeared to the other end of the bar.

Adam shrugged, "Your brother really likes me, I can tell." He tipped his beer mug towards me and said, "Here's to life, love and the pursuit of art!"

"Cheers!" I clanked my mug to his. I drank down half my beer and excused myself to go to the ladies room. I was hyperventilating. I ducked into one of the tiny gray stalls and shook five Valiums into my hand. I swallowed them dry. Frantically searching my purse for a paper bag to breathe into, I spun around in the stall. I grabbed one of those little disposable paper bags for sanitary napkins and tried breathing in it. I laughed, then shook out five more V's, choked them back, and sat on the toilet with my head between my knees; and the little bag scrunched over my nose and mouth. The bag crinkled in and out as my breath slowed . . . I thought . . . about a lighthouse . . . and a pale blue sky . . . and the tide caressing the sandy sea shore . . . and the seabirds sailing ever so lightly on the warm breeze . . . and me and Adam Sault breathing in unison as we embraced in the perfect kiss . . . .

I flushed the toilet. I felt hallowed.

Adam chuckled when I came back, "I thought you drowned in there."

I slid onto the bar stool and gulped down the rest of my beer. I started feeling lighter, and smiled at him for the first time and asked, "You want another one? I'm buying."

"Well, yes. Thank you."

I reached over to the tap behind the bar and poured two more mugs.

"So tell me, Eve White, did you learn anything in my class?"

"That sounds like a loaded question," I said.

"No, I'm serious. Most of the students I teach really have no interest in art at all. And the ones that do, often don't have the talent to become artists."

"Well, I don't know what category that puts me in. I think of myself as an artist, even though I work in a cookie factory."

"Are you still going to school?"

"Yeah ... I'm taking a painting class now." I lied. (I lied because I didn't want him to think that his art class was the sum total of my artistic experience.)

"Really? Do you have Camden?"

Why is it, I'm wondering, that people ask you REALLY? Do they REALLY think you're just babbling in a delirium, and you're not sure what you've said? I checked with the deceit mode on my mental computer ... if I answered the question

"no," then he would ask me who my teacher was; if I said I didn't know, or if I made up a name, he would know I was lying. So I said, "Ah, yeah I have Camden."

"How do you like her?"

"Um ... I like her ... She's ... (My great computer was searching for an appropriate response. It was having some technical difficulties assimilating this new program. I alternated to a blank screen and began to create.) She's very emphatic. You know, she really concentrates on balance and movement, and at the same time she sneaks in little tidbits of technique."

"Really?" he asked again, "I think she's a witch and she should have retired five years ago. But that's probably a personal bias on my part. She's friendly with my ex-wife who no longer speaks to me."

I wanted to probe the ex-wife situation. I wanted to query the absence of Tina B-M-O. My computer wouldn't let me. Adam Sault was slipping away. I didn't want him thinking about the painful memories of his marriage. But I didn't want him to know how badly I wanted him either. My mouth opened. I said something and he laughed. I laughed and drank the rest of my beer down. I asked him if he wanted another.

"Well one more, OK. Then, if you'd like, we can take a walk over to my place. I just live up the street, and I'll show you the *Creation* I've been working on for the last two years."

I nodded my head up and down like I was having seizure. "Yessss!" I said like he had just touched my forbidden zone. I poured us two more beers and asked, "What kind of *Creation* are you creating?"

"Well it's not an entirely new concept, but I'm combining painting and photography. I started it when I was still married, and my wife didn't like it very much . . . So she gave me the Old Tomato."

"What's the Old Tomato?"

"The ultimatum; stop this now, or get a divorce."

"I really think that married couples should be more supportive of each other's individual pursuits," I said, starting to blather. "I went with a guy once who was really jealous of everything that I did without him. That kind of relationship is really stifling. I really think that artists need more breathing room than other people, don't you?" I asked, hoping to shut down my rambling mode.

"Yeah, it was something like that." He tipped his mug up and licked his dewy lips. "Well I'm ready when you are."

I slid off my barstool like a scoop of ice cream. I plopped onto the floor and melted out the door with Adam Sault's arm around me.

It had stopped raining, and we strolled casually-slow. The extra-extra Valium I'd taken had made my eyes kind of misty and the street looked as if it were covered with sparkling gems. "Doesn't the pavement come to life after it rains?" I said.

He smiled. His eyes reflected a zillion points of light, the gems on the street, the haze of the street lamps, the orange blinking turn signal of a cab at the next corner. I was falling into his eyes, beyond the stars, beyond the known galaxy of thought.

I held onto his arm, and he just kind of wheeled me along. "Most people don't see things like this, Eve. Most people are just put out by the rain and never really open their eyes to see the rainbow of life."

We turned the corner, and he steered me across the street. He pulled a key ring out of his pocket, deftly twirled the ring around, and with one smooth motion unlocked the security door to his building. It swung open like the door to my heart. I sort of fell inside the stairway because he had let go of me, and the vitamin V seemed to have a concentrated effect on my knees.

"Are you OK to walk up the stairs?" he asked me.

I looked up at the gravity waves which zig-zagged in a confusing pattern. The anti-gravity mode in my brain chuckled at me. I put one foot on the first step and it slid right back to the ground. I held my hand out to Adam, "How far up?" I asked.

"C'mon you can do it." He took my hand and I seemed to float to the top of the building. I bobbed in front of his door like a marshmallow lost at sea. He tugged me inside and clicked on a light switch. One blue spotlight went on over my head. He flicked another switch and a red light went on about a foot over. Then a yellow. He kept flicking switches until this vast loft space was trembling with colored orbs.

Large furniture-type objects were strategically placed throughout the space on top of platforms looking much like fragments of thought. A powder-blue bentwood rocking-chair was perched in an artificial corner, a corner that was created by a white fishnet. Another platform had a ball-and-claw-foot bathtub on it with a window frame hanging over it. The window frame had double-faced mirrors in it and was suspended from the ceiling with wire. I stood there with my mouth hanging open. I said, "WOW!" Honest.

Adam Sault took me by the hand and floated me through his space. At the farthest end of the loft was an empty platform with a large white canvas looming above it. This meant something.

I gazed at this empty white cloth and felt myself being sucked into it. This definitely meant something. "What is this?" I asked and pointed at it.

"This is my *Creation!*" he beamed.

I looked at him very puzzled. "Your wife wanted a divorce because of this?" I asked.

"Not exactly. It's not quite finished yet." He stepped behind the canvas and switched on a light, which made the fabric appear to glow. He floated back into view with a bottle of red wine and two blue ceramic chalices.

"I really don't think I can drink any wine," I said.

"Ah, but this is magic wine. This is very gentle to the mind and body." He uncorked the bottle and tipped it gracefully to the edge of each cup, then sat down on the platform. I was still standing. (Imagine that.) He reached out and touched my cheek. "You have something very special, Eve."

"I do?"

"You have a very rare essence on your face, a kind of mixture of innocence and instinct."

"I do?"

His fingers traced my cheekbone lightly and trailed down my neck. I sighed. I moved closer and felt myself sinking. He put his warm arms around me. He breathed in my ear, "I want you."

I squirmed out of his heavenly hold. "I'm really tired," I muttered.

He reached beneath the platform and pulled out a fat white satin pillow. "Here, lay your head down," he said.

I stretched out like Sleeping Beauty. He went for my throat. His beard tickled. I giggled. He stroked my face and neck with his velvet hands, and circled my breasts with the electric vibration of his trembling fingers. He teased my mouth open with tiny licks of his firm tongue, and began sliding in and out of the tight O of my quivering lips.

He sat up and looked at me as if I were a rare flower. "You are incredibly beautiful," he whispered. "I want to paint you. I want to capture your essence on film. Have you ever been professionally photographed?"

"Only for school pictures."

"Would you let me take your picture?"

"As long as I don't have to sit up," I laughed.

He glided behind the canvas and came back with a camera on a tripod. He altered some of the spotlights and then sat down next to me with a hair brush. "Will you let me brush your hair?" he asked as he took off my Budweiser cap and pulled the rubber band out of my ponytail. I was too tired to consider whether I had any options. He pulled me up by my shoulders and began gently brushing my lifeless mane till it gleamed. "You are so special," he whispered, "Why do you hide under that hat?"

"Um . . . I don't know . . . just habit I guess . . . I wear it at work."

"When you see yourself in my pictures, Eve, you'll see how truly beautiful you are. Someone like you should not go unnoticed." He stepped behind the camera and twisted the lens and started clicking away. I stared into the black hole of the lens. I was being tugged in with every little twitch of the shutter.

Adam stopped shooting and said, "You look a little tense, here . . ." he said, pouring me another glass of wine.

Tense? I'm thinking, if I were any more relaxed I'd be lying in a casket holding a lily. I sipped on the wine and said,

"I guess I just don't know how to respond. I've never done this before."

"Just relax. You're a natural. Trust me." He leaned over and kissed my ear. My neck. My lips. My head crashed back onto the pillow. He unbuttoned the top button of my flannel shirt. I sighed. I gulped. "I want to touch your breasts," he breathed and looked at me for permission.

I stretched my arms up over my head and arched my chest towards his face. He gingerly unbuttoned, and pulled my shirt back around my shoulders. He began rubbing his beard over my rising pink flesh. I stared in awe as if I had never been naked in my life. I was Eve and he was Adam and we had just discovered the sweet fruit.

Adam Sault was seeing me for the first time. In his heart, he must know that I'm the one who sent him the poetry, but his mind has not made the connection. All he knows is this divine feeling that he **must** experience my love. We are fused in this moment of awareness. He tugged. He licked. He sucked. He disappeared behind the camera again and began flicking away. "Yesss . . . Yesss," he was muttering. "You are perfect!"

I was floating. I was perfect. I was confirmed. I was BONA FIDE! I hardly noticed Adam unzipping my jeans and saying that he wanted ALL OF ME. I wouldn't let him take my purple socks off. I told him my feet were cold.

He stood next to me like a statue. I reached over and unbuttoned his shirt. He was hairy. Very. I ran my fingers through the silky fur of his chest, down his soft stomach which hollowed in around his jutting hip bones. I reached down and slid my hand between his thighs and pushed. He took a deep breath. "Would you let me paint you, Eve?" he wheezed.

I looked at him curiously. I felt my head nodding yes. He reached beneath the platform and pulled out a black box. I rolled on my side and watched as he laid out tubes of acrylic paint, brushes, a pallet, a jug of water, a jar, rags . . . and he began telling me that I was the perfect canvas and that together we were going to create a masterpiece that would set the modern art world on its ear.

He poured me another glass of wine, and I was spilling out into the realm beyond ecstasy. I was floating just slightly above my body, half-in, half-out, experiencing a duality. Feeling the immensity of creation. I could see with every pore of my being.

Adam Sault kissed me gently, all over. He squeezed some bright red paint onto the pallet and selected a long thin brush, which he dipped in the jar of water and then into the paint. He smiled at me and said, "Don't worry, luv, I'll wash it off you later."

He made thin, tiny, swirling designs on one side of my face and curled the pattern down around my breasts. He dabbed so lightly. It tickled so nicely. He dabbed blue and pink little breath-like wisps of thought. Little poems danced across my flesh like fairies. Little fronds of love caressed my bare soul.

This was his gift to me. This tender touch of the soul was Adam's words, the words he was unable to speak, the words he'd longed for all his life. He had finally found his voice in me. My poems had fused with his inner being, and he didn't even know it was me. This was perfection!

I was in a total trance by the time he reached the joint of my hips and carefully lifted up my left knee so that my legs were just barely parted. He picked up a slightly bigger, and only slightly stiffer paintbrush and dipped it in the water. He dabbed me ... pulsingly ... with the wet brush ... He teased me. He stroked me. He brushed the bud of my heavenly apple-blossom until I burst into full bloom! Ah, the sweetest fruit in the garden! He feasted!

There were miniature leopard spots and tiny tiger stripes and swirling curlicue designs painted in patches all over me. I was tattooed with the velvety brush of love. Adam was moving the camera around and covering every angle (almost). He told me that his vision had been of me all along. He said he was going to enlarge the photos to poster size and then he was going to paint designs on the empty spaces of my skin, right onto the photos. He showed me one that he had started doing of his wife, but he said that she was all wrong for the composition. She didn't have any animal-innocence, he said.

As he stroked away with his paintbrush adding dashes here and there, he kept telling me how perfect I was and how he felt so complete in this experience, and so on. I was bobbing up and down and in and out of my body. I was almost asleep, when I felt him tug my socks off. He stared. His jaw dropped like a broken draw-bridge. He shuddered. I spread my toes out wide.

He set his camera aside. I sat up straight. "What's wrong?" I smiled.

"Um . . . your feet . . . Um . . ."

"Yes, those are my feet." I wiggled my toes so he could get the full effect.

He half laughed, "You have webbed feet."

"You have good eyes," I chirped.

"I'm . . . sorry . . . it just really . . . looks . . . awful."

"Awful?" I cocked my head.

"Well, I mean . . . haven't you ever . . . I mean . . . can't they fix that . . . surgically or something?" He looked away.

"Fix what?"

"I mean . . . It just doesn't look right . . . I mean . . . It kind of ruins the rest of the pictures. Have you thought about . . . seeing a doctor . . . I mean . . . I . . . just . . . there must be something they can do."

"I thought you wanted something special?"

"Well I do, but . . . I want it to look . . . real . . . at least . . . human."

I stared at him. Who was this? This cannot be the same person whom I sent my deepest thoughts to. Who was this? This cannot be the man who was living every waking moment wondering who I was and why I was sharing my love with him. Who was this? This cannot be my destiny. THIS CANNOT BE HAPPENING TO ME!

I was confused. How could my Adam Sault be cruel? How could he profess his love for me with each brush stroke, and then in the next breath become repulsed by his own perception?

I pulled my body and spirit together. I pulled my socks on. I pulled my jeans and flannel shirt on. Adam tried to say he was sorry or something like that. I bolted out the door into the black morning with my gym shoes in one hand and my Budweiser cap in the other. I ran through the streets snivelling, and finally threw myself onto a park bench and sobbed my eyeballs out. I ripped off my socks and wiggled my toes. I petted my toes. My feet were exactly the way they were supposed to be.

I walked in the rain for about an hour. I wished that Adam Sault would die. Disappear from life. Vacate from my thoughts. How could I be so naive? How could I be beaten at my own game? How could I be pulverized by my own imagination? This just wasn't real.

I dragged my torn heart home and stood in the shower as my multicolored fantasy swirled down the drain. I was Zoned. If my imagination had the power to invert my own life so tragically, I pondered . . . what if . . . ?

THIRTY-TWO

Dr. Marvin said that behavior modification was the key to my self-imposed prison, and that if I could discipline myself to observe my potential lovers before I got involved with them, then I would be free from emotional bondage.

I say, we are never more discontented then when we wrestle with our own invitations.

"What's that supposed to mean?" Pup asks me.

I hold her hand even though hand-holding and other displays of affection are not permitted in prison. "What that means," I tell her, "is that we know who we are, and yet we find being human unacceptable."

She rolls her eyes. "What does being human have to do with invitations? Why the hell don't you speak English?"

"Words can only scratch the surface of the soul," I tell her. "I can talk to you till time stands still, and you still won't understand what timelessness is.

"The word invitation," I say, "is merely an enticement for you and by your own invocation to rise above the private hell in which you've imprisoned your own heart."

Pup looks up at me with her lost eyes. "You know who I feel most sorry for?"

"Who?" I ask.

"That poor doctor who had to listen to you droning on and on like this for over a year. The guy is probably strapped down to a bed in the loony bin right about now babbling incoherently."

I don't feel sorry for Dr. Marvin. I don't feel sorry for Adam Sault. I don't feel sorry for Pup. I don't feel sorry for myself. Sorry is a word that implies wretchedness. I ask you, is not wretchedness a state of feeling? Is not art beyond the mere emotional dimension of feeling?

One of Adam Sault's favorite sayings to his drawing students was, "A picture says a thousand words." He would expound at length on how important every detail, every movement, and every dot on the paper meant something. But I say, a picture is beyond words. Words are thought, and pure art is expression which transcends language.

Dr. Marvin liked to challenge my artistic theories. He asked me why I wrote poetry if words were obviously so inferior to visual art.

"They're not inferior to visual art, Doc. They're another realm of art, altogether."

"But you insist that words have boundaries and that art does not. How can they both be art?"

Dr. Marvin helped push me. If he had not been so immature as to dispute my every philosophical diversion, I might never have run out of theories and hence, I might never have shut up and listened to the Sandman.

"Lisssennn . . ." said the Sandman.

I was at the laundromat. It had been a week since my artistic excursion with Adam Sault. I was pondering inversion. I was contemplating original sin. I was ruminating the possibility that the whole Garden of Eden facade was concocted by Adam because he felt guilty. If the serpent is symbolic of the phallus, then it was really Adam who tempted Eve. And I'll bet it wasn't an apple he was tempting her to eat either!

Was it possible that now was the time to settle the score? Was it possible that Adam had felt ashamed after he had spent his seed into Eve's forbidden cavity? The problem with whole story was that, without having eaten the fruit from the tree of knowledge, Adam and Eve would have been too unknowledgeable to understand what God meant when he allegedly forbade them to indulge. I can hear Adam saying, "Hey Eve, let's do every thing until we find out what DON'T means!" I wondered if Eve had had webbed feet. I wondered if Adam had thought that she should ask God to FIX them.

"Lisssennn . . ." the Sandman whispered again. I was plugged into the yellow plastic chair. Sipping a Diet Coke. Watching the underwear tumble casually. Just barely breathing. When a swirl of golden dust spun before my eyes.

"Lisssennn . . ." his voice tempted me.

I was still in my body. It was very confusing to hear such a voice while I was still in my body. "Follow me . . . ." the voice said and it spun towards a washing machine with the lid up. It hovered there.

I stood up like a sleepwalker with my arms straight out in front of me and shuffled over to the machine. The shimmering Sandman slipped down into the bottom of the machine and called my name. "EEEEVE!" I stuck my head inside of the machine. There was a huge red apple inside. The Sandman said, "Give this gift to Adam and you will understand what gifts he has given to you."

I lifted the apple out of the washer and shuffled back to my yellow plastic chair. The other patrons of the laundromat just stared at me. I took a sip of my Diet Coke and smiled politely.

This could be the great redemption, I thought. The Sandman could be the spirit of the original Adam making amends for the sins of his first life. Adam Sault could be the karmic monster which Adam No.1 had let run amok since the days in the garden. This could be the evolutionary pivot point for our original father. THIS COULD CHANGE THE DESTINY OF THE WORLD!

I didn't know that the apple was poisoned. Honest. All I knew was that I had to deliver it, and that I had to tempt Adam Sault into taking a bite. This was not going to be easy I thought, since he was probably on the brink of total paranoia because of the final poem I had sent him.

THIRTY-THREE

The prosecuting attorney objected to my disclosure about where the poisoned apple came from. I had said I didn't know. He suggested that I should be reevaluated for psychological instability. I told Ol' Randy Boy Perkins "NO WAY!" I didn't want to spend the next fifteen years in the loony bin. He said I would get out of the bin quicker with good behavior than I would get out of prison, but there was a stronger possibility that I'd go crazy there and never get out.

Dr. Marvin remained cool and professional throughout the prosecutor's badgering. I really thought Dr. Marvin's testimony would help me because:

A) He was a highly respected psychiatrist in the community, with over 20 years of dedicated service.

B) His professional opinion was that I was incapable of premeditated murder.

C) He thought I was writing the poetry for him.

The prosecuting attorney gave me the chills. He had frosty silver hair and ice blue eyes. He wore gun metal gray suits and polished steel-rimmed glasses that seemed to lock his discerned brow into frozen competency. He posed with one hand on the Bible in front of Dr. Marvin. "Would you tell the court exactly what was the therapeutic value of Ms. White's poetry."

"Ms. White was having difficulty expressing her emotions," Dr. Marvin said. "She was suffering from an acute anxiety disorder, and in my professional experience most anxiety issues can be resolved by confrontation. I felt that her poetry was a means for her to confront the anxieties."

"She never told you that she had mailed the poems to Mr. Sault?"

"No."

"Where you aware of her obsession with Adam Sault?"

"No."

"Did you ever have a sexual encounter with the defendant?"

Randall Perkins bellowed, "Objection, Your Honor!"

"Overruled," the judge moaned. "Please answer the question."

"No."

"During the year and a half she was under your *close* scrutiny, did Ms. White ever attempt to seduce you or suggest a sexual encounter?"

"No, she did not."

"Tell us then, Dr. Marvin, what did your therapy consist of other than poetry reading?"

Perkins thrust a bony finger toward the bench to object, but seemed to change his mind mid-thought.

"Ms. White had a lot of unresolved issues from her childhood and feelings of insecurity, which, having been suppressed for so long, were creating an illusory response to normal living. We worked together to help her deal more effectively with her abnormal emotional responses."

"So you talked. How nice. You read poetry . . . how nice. Did it ever occur to you, Dr. Marvin, that Ms. White was significantly more disturbed than your average neurotic?"

Randall Perkins opened his mouth but nothing came out.

"The manifestations of Ms. White's anxiety disorder were quite common," Dr. Marvin stated.

"Is MURDER a common manifestation of anxiety disorder?"

"OBJECTION!" Perkins finally blurted out.

The judge looked startled by the outburst. He nodded at the D.A. "Please rephrase the question."

"In your twenty-plus years as a psychiatrist, Dr. Marvin, have you ever seen a person with ACUTE ANXIETY DISORDER (he screamed) LOSE CONTROL?"

"OBJECTION!" Perkins tooted, "Leading the witness."

The judge overruled and the D.A. bludgeoned Dr. Marvin with a series of questions about the therapeutic values of vitamin V.

"The drug Valium, which you prescribed for Ms. White's . . . anxiety attacks, is considered relatively safe when used as prescribed. Correct?"

"Yes."

"Were you aware that Ms. White was also drinking alcohol while she was under your *close* scrutiny?"

"Ms. White told me that she drank a beer occasionally, which I did not deem abusive."

"And what are some of the side effects of Valium when it is mixed with alcohol?"

"Excessive drowsiness, lightheadedness and depression."

"What about memory loss? Isn't that possible too?"

"Yes, memory loss is possible."

"What about violent outbursts? Isn't that possible too?"

"Yes that's possible, but not very common."

"Isn't it possible, Dr. Marvin, that Eve White, while under the influence of alcohol and Valium, lost control of her faculties. And out of her rage at Adam Sault for rejecting her, (he paused, spun on his heels, and stared at me) decided that killing him would end her obsession?"

Dr. Marvin was cool. "Sir, that is possible. But it is equally possible that Eve White had nothing to do with the murder."

The D.A. slit a smile at the jury. "I have no further questions at this time."

THIRTY-FOUR

I stayed locked in my room for two days after my artistic excursion with Adam Sault. The darkness swallowed me. The shadows gnawed on the raw edges of my heart. The silence stampeded through my head like herd of hippopotamus. I swallowed many V's hoping to sleep.

My paper dream . . . My artistic theories . . . Somehow it all meant something . . . Somehow it all made sense . . . There was a rhythm . . . A pattern . . . A texture . . . A precarious balance . . . I was the pivot point . . . I was the Great Mother . . . I was the Key Master . . . I had the answers . . . . But the questions danced in phantasmic circles around me.

It was a paper dream, I told myself. An art attack. My inside was seeping out, all over the paper. It had to happen this way.

Only words seemed to ease the pain.

Only words seemed to exacerbate my grim perceptions.

I felt rage for the first time in my life. I felt mutilated. I felt sorry for Adam Sault but I couldn't let him escape from my heart unscathed. My brain was burning in its inner friction.

It was against even my flimsy values to kill a human being. But I wanted him to die an emotional death.

I couldn't possibly tell him that I was "*Severely Yours.*" The whole creation of our love was based upon my belief that love is more powerful than lust. I was tricked by my own lust! I couldn't see past my own desire. I saw only the physical beauty of Adam Sault, and in the process of renouncing my aspirations, I transferred my energies. I had expected Adam Sault to do something that I was incapable of doing myself. I was the one who was judging from the outside.

I wallowed in my pain. It wasn't fair that I—I who had struggled so hard to find the truth—I who had suffered more chagrin than any woman had ever endured—it just wasn't fair that I should pay the price alone. Adam Sault should know that I'm hurting. He should put the fucking pieces together and figure out that I was the genius sending him those divine words.

I remembered the word, ACTION. It still had an optimistic tone. I remembered thinking about how Adam Sault must feel as he read each one of my poems.

"ACTION!" I said between my sobs. ACTION would at least make Adam Sault feel sorry for the way he hurt me. "ACTION!" I sobbed, as I wrote his final poem.

I'm Going To Kill You

>   Beware this poisonous paper.
> Beware that strangers will deliver.
>   Beware of the silent gift
> when darkness opens your door.
>   Beware of the ripe fruit.
> Beware of the painted angel.
>   Beware of your thoughts
> for fear will destroy you.

>   Severely Yours!

I sealed the envelope and felt relieved. I wanted to Zone Adam Sault. That's all. I wanted him to be aware that every action has certain responsibilities. I mailed the poem to Adam Sault on my way to work that Monday. I had an appointment with Dr. Marvin that evening and he asked me how everything had gone in the last week.

I said, "Everything's dandy, Doc, except I had O.B.E. at work again today."

"What happened?"

"I had just put a batch of butter cookies in the oven. I set the timer, and ran to the john. I have my routine down to a science and I knew I had exactly seven minutes before I had to take out the last tray I had put in. And I have my toilet routine down to a science, too, so I knew I had time to smoke a half a cigarette. So I lit up and sat down on the cool seat and then, just sort of went into a trance, watching my cigarette smoke swirl up to the vent. And there I went right with it."

Dr. Marvin scribbled his notes. "And where did you go?"

"I sailed up through the vent system and out onto the roof. And ... the Sandman was there ... it was as if he were calling me. He was hovering over a smokestack ... just sort of swirling there ... Then he disappeared."

"What did you do then?"

"I sailed back down to my body and ran back out to the oven. Jose, one of the dough boys, had tried to rescue the cookies, but it was too late. They were burnt."

"And how did that make you feel?"

I thought for a whole second how absurd Dr. Marvin's questions were. I looked at him dead seriously and said, "Like a fish out of jello." Then I busted up laughing. I lost momentary control of my deceit mode. I snorted. I howled. I hooted. Tears were squirting from my eyes.

Dr. Marvin looked confused.

I grabbed the box of Kleenex and held it out to Dr. Marvin, which I thought, was even funnier. I was getting dizzy, forgetting to breathe. I blew my nose real loud and fell back into my chair with a long, satisfied sigh.

Dr. Marvin smiled professionally. "Are you feeling better this week?" he asked, and flipped through his notes. "Last week we were discussing your submissive behavior and the way it makes you feel to be controlled within a relationship."

I studied Dr. Marvin's tie. It was pale yellow with tiny burgundy diamonds. I could see my hands trembling as they tightened the knot ... as the doctor's docile face began to contort ... as his fat tongue bulged out of his mouth ... as thick red blood began gurgling in the back of his throat ... as the fresh red blood splattered down onto his lovely tie. I looked up at him and said, "If I consent to submission, then what power have I surrendered?"

"How about your power to make your own happiness?"

Dr. Marvin believed that happiness was a matter of method. He said that I denied myself the power to make my own happiness by surrendering to the happiness that others could give me.

But I say, happiness is not something you get from other people. It's not something you attain with control. It's not the pot of gold at the end of the rainbow. Happiness is the rainbow. Happiness is the transient moments of awareness of the interdependency of the rain, the sun, the eyes, the brain, the heart, the inside seeping out, the outside seeping in, the fusion of experience with experiencer, the knowing brush of the untouchable . . . the gentle bumping of souls. That's all.

THIRTY-FIVE

The prosecuting attorney read the poem, "I'm Going to Kill You" out loud. I was at the stand innocently playing with the tassels on my shawl. The D.A. spat at me, "You would like the jury to believe that this letter was intended only to scare Adam Sault, and that you had no thoughts of murdering him when you wrote this?"

"It was intended to *Zone* him," I said. "That's all. He was supposed to be so afraid, that in his self-absorbed state of panic he would overreact to a point that he would hurt himself . . . emotionally speaking."

"And so a week later when you realized that he was not reacting as you had intended, you decided to help him along by delivering a poisoned apple to his door, DIDN'T YOU, MS. WHITE?"

I glared at the D.A. (Oh, what a wormy world we live in!) I glared at Perkins who was cleaning under his fingernails with a paper clip. I glared at Robert who sat like a plastic holy statue, unaffected. "No . . . I don't . . . I didn't . . . I don't remember," I mumbled and started to snivel.

The evidence was stacked, mounted, and heaped against me. I was seen on the night of the murder, at Eden's Gate with a basket of apples. Adam Sault had photos of our affair hung up all over his dark room. The poem, "I'm Going to Kill You" was clenched in his hand as he collapsed almost instantly upon taking a bite of the apple. Tina B-M-O had identified me from the photos. The police came to arrest me at the cookie factory. I promptly fainted. And even though Dr. Marvin, Jooly Jones, and Robert all testified that I was harmless, the fact was that I did deliver the apple. It was my role in the great cosmic inversion. It was my contribution to the continuum of the artistic panorama. I had to do it. And the jury had to find me guilty.

The jury was limited in their understanding of the bigger picture. They didn't know that justice had already been served. The jury perceived murder as a crime and not as a natural phenomenon occurring spontaneously within the realm of art.

I ask you, where do the laws of man end and the laws of nature begin? Is not the perfect beauty of the universe in direct proportion to our inability to control it?

I was at Eden's Gate with the basket of apples. I was waiting for Adam Sault to come slithering in. I saw Tina B-M-O and figured that she must be waiting for him too. When she left, I followed her, but she didn't turn down his street. I approached Adam's building casually. Before I buzzed his number, I looked around. The street was void of human life. A black cat tiptoed silently down the sidewalk and stopped to watch me. I wondered if it might be the reincarnation of my Cosmic Cat Brother, Ernie Stone, pausing to witness another Zoning. I took the great red apple that I had kept in my purse and placed it strategically in the basket. I buzzed number three. A moment later the door was buzzing, so I pulled it open. I didn't float up the stairs this time. I sort of moved robotically as if I were programmed to do this and had no will of my own. The door was open a crack so I stuck my head in. "Hello" I said, and my voice echoed through the colored-orb-lit space.

"C'mon in," Adam said as he appeared from behind a platform with a brass bed on top of it. He was wearing a white terry cloth bathrobe. His hair was wet. His eyes popped when he saw me. He said, "Eve?"

I said, "Hi."

He stammered and backed up a few steps. "Um . . . I . . . Um . . . was expecting somebody else."

"I won't stay long," I said. "I just have been thinking about what happened and I wanted to talk to you."

He relaxed a bit. "OK, um . . . you want something to drink?"

"No. I just feel really bad about leaving here in a huff and I sort of want to apologize."

"Hey, I'm the one who should feel bad. I shouldn't have hurt your feelings like that. That was really an asinine thing to say, and I'm really sorry."

He reached out to embrace me. I let him. His bathrobe smelled like baby powder.

"Listen," I said, "I guess I better go before your guest arrives."

He pulled back a little and looked at his watch. "It's late, she's probably not coming now."

"Your girlfriend?" I asked.

"Actually, she's an ex-girlfriend. She won't take no for an answer. She and my ex-wife have been harassing me, sort of. So I asked her to come over tonight, just to talk."

"What do you mean, harassing you?" I asked.

"It's kind of silly," he said, "but she's been sending me poetry and weird things in the mail ever since we broke up, and not signing her name," he paused. "It's like she's trying to get me to change my mind about her, so that she can turn around, and then give it back to me."

"Really?" I said.

"Really," he replied. "Like I said it's kind of silly, but she sent a real nasty letter last week, and I asked her to come over tonight, just to talk."

I looked up at Adam's Adam's apple. It looked ripe. I asked, "If she didn't sign them, how do you know it was her?"

"Take a seat and I'll show you." He pointed up the three stairs of the platform leading to the brass bed. I stepped up as he walked across the room and pulled a cardboard box out from under a platform, and then carried it over to the bed. He put the box at the foot of the bed and unfolded the top. My poems were in it. I felt my face burning red and my ears burning purple, about to ignite my hair. What am I gonna say now?

"Listen to this," he said as he opened one of the envelopes. He began reading "In Time."

I shuddered. "Can I see that?" I asked.

"Sure." He handed it to me.

I read carefully, as if I were understanding my own words for the first time.

In Time

In time
>you will not know me
for my heart
>is beyond time

In time
>we have found
one moment
>of timelessness

>>>>>Severely, Yours

I turned the poem over as if I were looking for a clue on the back. "So, what does it mean?" I asked boldly.

"It means that she's got some emotional problems."

"I see. But how do you know that your old girlfriend's the one who wrote it? I mean, it's typewritten, it could be anybody."

He laughed, "Only Tina could write something this pathetic." He laughed again.

My brain began to boil and make gurgling noises inside my purple ears. He thought my poetry was pathetic. This was it. ACTION. I took two apples out of the basket and began shining them on my shirt. "Well," I said, "if her poetry was so PATH-ET-IC, then why did you keep it all?"

He laughed a little and said, "Well, I guess it intrigued me a little bit." He reached into the pocket of his bathrobe and pulled out a folded piece of paper. "But this one she sent me last week was less than inspiring."

As he unfolded the white crackling paper I caught his eyes again. I caught them and kept them as I held the apples out towards him.

"You want one?" I said, dangling the big red beauties in front of his hungry eyes.

He seemed to look inside me for nourishment. I remembered Elvis at Blue Lake. I remembered that Elvis had known exactly what the apples were all about and how to get me to eat them. "Which one of these apples looks sweeter to you?" I asked.

He chuckled, "They look the same to me."

"What if I told you that one of these apples was a rare hybrid that is grown exclusively in one tiny orchard in Blue Lake, Michigan, and that it is the sweetest fruit known to mankind?"

He shrugged his shoulders. "Well, you're the expert I guess, cause they look the same to me."

"If you're going to eat the apple . . . Adam . . . then doesn't that make you the expert?"

I studied his face. He looked as if he had hungered for this moment his entire life. He took the Granny-Mac-Blue. He took a lavish bite and then another. I laughed. He gurgled. "This is sour!" he mumbled and his eyes began to water.

It happened so fast. He seemed to just stop breathing and he fell back on the bed. I looked down at him. Tears fell down his lovely cheeks as he gasped and curled up in a fetal ball. Clutching the poem in one hand he let the apple roll on to the bed. It seemed so familiar. Like a famous painting I'd seen a zillion times. Like a picture postcard passed down through time.

The coroner's report noted that: The ingested portion of the apple contained over 400 milligrams of highly concentrated liquid puffer fish toxin. (100 milligrams is a lethal dose.) The subject almost instantly experienced respiratory failure.

When Pokey whacked off her husband's head with a machete she tells me, "It was already written that way. It was like I was water, flowing into the great sea. Water knows its destiny."

Dr. Marvin had asked me a zillion times what I wanted to do with my life. He said that I needed a sense of direction. But I say, like Pokey says, once you realize that you are fluid in the great pool of inversion you simply let it flow. You can't fight the rain with a fire.

THIRTY-SIX

I left my body during the sentencing. I was convicted of premeditated murder. Randall Perkins said they let me off pretty easy with fifteen years, and parole eligibility in eight years.

They took me in a paddy wagon to the State Correctional Facility for Women. The building looked like a giant metal farm. I started shivering as they led me and three other prisoners up the sidewalk with our ankles chained and our wrists cuffed. There were at least ten guns pointed at us and ready to pop our little heads off if we had decided to protest.

We shuffled inside, and my heart caved in as the steel door echoed shut on my past. I was getting dizzy. The gray floor rolled out in front of me like a giant stretcher. I fell onto it, ready to be taken to the morgue. A guard grabbed my handcuffs and jerked me back up to my feet. I looked through her. She had black-glass eyes. There was a fire burning in her brain. A bonfire. She was going to sacrifice me to the flames. She hissed at me as she dragged me down the tunnel to hell.

I was shoved into a brightly lit office and led to a desk. The woman at the desk ordered me to sit down. I wanted to leave my body. I wasn't sure if I was having an I.B.E. or if these people were really servants of Satan.

I looked around for the other prisoners that I had come in with. There was no trace of them. I presumed that they had already been incinerated, and that their crimes were probably much more heinous than mine. Yes, they wanted me to pay penance. They wanted to peel my eyeballs and scratch foul words in my ivory flesh. The woman at the desk was sorting my papers and asking me questions about my place of birth, my parents, and allergies, et cetera. It occurred to me that I needed some vitamin V and I would be able to answer her questions without hesitation. I politely told her that I needed my medication, and she began to laugh uproariously. The guard standing next to me with the fireball eyes started howling with laughter, too. She jerked me up by the handcuffs again and started dragging me towards a wall with inches marked off on it. She shoved me up against the wall and growled, "Don't move an inch."

Another soldier came and placed a plate in my hands with numbers on it and they took some pictures. Fire-woman was really beginning to bug me so after the pictures when she jerked me by the wrists again (which were incidentally bleeding all over the floor) I took a deep breath and yanked my hands out of the cuffs, leaving half my skin hinged to the metal. I leapt up on top of a desk and screamed like a baboon.

I saw the ceiling flying by at a zillion miles an hour as my head crashed into a chair, a wall, and then the floor. My head bounced on the floor like a ball of cookie dough. The vibration was enough to send me shaking out of my body. I watched closely as they gathered round and poked at my flesh. Two, big, dopey-looking thugs came and lifted my sad heap onto a stretcher. They wheeled me away to another brightly lit room. They bandaged up my head and soaked my hands in some solution and wrapped them up tight. They lay me down on a mattress and pulled leather straps tightly over my arms, my waist, and my legs. I looked dead.

I popped back into my body and decided that if I were dead, I would not be able to accomplish this simple feat. I opened my eyes and felt a heavy throbbing in the corner of my brain. I turned my head and saw a young girl strapped down in the bed next to me. I mumbled, "Where am I?"

She moaned, "You're in second aid."

"Where?"

"You're in second aid, babe. They don't have first aid in prison."

"What happened?"

"To me or to you?"

"How did I get here?"

"Probably a case of mistaken identity. Happens a lot around here. Take me, for example. They think I stole fourteen Cadillacs, when in fact, the only evidence they had against me was that they caught me sleeping in one. That's awfully presumptuous, don'tcha think?"

I pondered for a minute. "I don't know," I said.

"My name's Pup," she said, "What's yours?"

I pondered for two minutes . . . "Um . . . Eve."

"Wow, that's a cool name. Is it short for something?"

"Yeah," I sniffed, "it's short for Evening."

"Your name is Evening?" she asked disbelievingly.

"No," I said. "I just thought that was funny."

Pup snickered, "Oh great, another comedian. So are you gonna tell me what you're in for, or do I have to squeeze it out of you?"

"I'm not really sure myself. I mean . . . I . . . It seems like a dream or a movie I'm watching . . . I don't really know . . . how . . . ."

"Is this your first conviction?"

"Yeah, I guess I was convicted . . . I just don't see how . . . I mean . . . It just doesn't seem real."

"What was the *alleged* crime?"

I pondered this for three minutes. "Murder, I guess. It's a long story."

"Well, you'll have at least six years to tell it."

"What?"

"Which word didn't you understand?"

I pondered this for many minutes. My poor little head was swimming with all this new data.

I asked Pup why she was in second aid. She said, "Because I'm dangerous to myself and to the well being of the other inmates."

I was taken from second aid to the hole. The hole is eight feet by eight feet. It has a toilet. It has a dim light that is turned off and on at strange intervals. It has a little steel window that is opened at strange intervals and peered into by strange eyes. It has a slot at the bottom of the door where strange sustenance is slid in on trays at strange intervals.

When they bolted the hole shut I felt peaceful. The trays came under the door and I just lay curled up in a ball on the smelly blanket. I watched the light go off and on. I watched the eyeballs burning through me. I needed my medication. I needed to sleep. I needed to sleep forever. I cried for medication. The eyeballs rolled happily around in the phantom skulls. I was fading. Slipping in and out of my body. I was calling to the Sandman. Who was the Sandman? Why did he set me up with a poisoned apple? Why did he do it? Where was his body? Was the Sandman real? Was Dr. Marvin right? Was I crazy?

I screamed and howled for the Sandman. But he was gone. He had been redeemed. He had used me the way Adam had used Eve in the garden. I had thought that the Sandman was my father, or my brother. I had thought that maybe my brother was trying to protect me as always, from my own ignorance. I thought that Dr. Marvin was hot on the trail of the Sandman when he suggested that it was my projected image of my father. I had thought that all the pieces would fit into place. I always thought like that. I always wrote such boring and predictable scripts for myself and the universe never complied.

Adam Sault's script was so easy to follow. I sent him all the information he needed in order to master his role. He could have been a star and wallowed eternally in the slick pit of my seduction. Instead he chose the dirt. He chose the black wormy world.

I screamed for medication. I wailed for the Sandman. I moaned for Divine Intervention. I heard a voice, an echo, a voice like my father's, or was it my mother's, or was Jooly's? The words hissed in my ear: "Because you have done this, cursed are you above all cattle, and above all wild animals, upon your belly you shall go, and dust shall you eat all the days of your life."

Was this clarification? Was there a God telling me that Adam Sault indeed had been reincarnated as a worm? Was my father behind all of this? Was the melodramatic phenomenon of my entire life simply a rationalization of my infantile ego? Was I merely a martyr for art?

Why did I tell Dr. Marvin that I was attracted to tall, dark, bearded, horny, and stupid men because they reminded me of Jesus? Was Dr. Marvin right? Was I trying to reunite with my father through spiritual osmosis? Was I trying to reunite Adam and Eve through my sexual intervention? Was I trying to give Adam his stupid rib back? Or was I a child of art?

Was art the disease that would destroy me like a cancer? Were artistic energies responsible for the "unnatural occurrences" in the Bible? Were those earliest writers as romantically delusional as I was?

The hole was getting darker. The need for vitamin V was like a fire burning me out of my brain; chasing me down the flaming corridors of terror. I was scratching my flesh trying to get out. My body was crawling with ants and lizards. There were worms writhing in my hair, and mushy noises in my ears. I began shaking out of my body. Jolting in and out with no will of my own. My body began convulsing. It threw me out like a broken-necked, Cuddly Duddly. It was screaming with stabbing pains at every nerve ending. It was pushing me away, heaving my soul out into the universe. It didn't want me anymore. MY BODY DIDN'T WANT ME ANYMORE!

I floated up towards the dim flashing overhead light. I felt my soul aching for tears, but with no eyes to shed them, I was frozen, locked in the pain. I began splitting into fragments, my very core melting and spilling up and out, swirling away from me. My soul was gasping for help as I was being tugged into the vast nothing.

My body didn't want me. There was no place to go, nothing to return to. The black hole sucked me in like a red JUJUBE. I plummeted through the black till I was empty. Hollow. Black to the black. Spiraling through eternity till I felt my soul dissolve. Fused with the seamless silence. Dead silence. Black silence. The silence which cannot be penetrated by sound.

Soullessly, I floated like a peaceful cloud of pond scum. Aimless. Mindless. Timeless.

This was love. This was the senseless, boundless dimension beyond the knowable parameters of consciousness. This was IT. The big IT. The inseparable IT. The forever IT. The IT that I am. The IT that all is. The IT of IT all!

During this moment of IT, I lost IT. A separation occurred suddenly, and I perceived a faint spark a zillion light years away. I drifted towards it by some strange gravitational tug. This was the light of inversion and I was ready to invert into whatever energy the universe needed me for. I began to twist and spin faster towards it, this pure white divine light. Suddenly it seemed, I cared. I wanted. I wanted to see and feel, to know what was the source of the light. I plummeted increasingly faster toward it. I crashed into it. It was a mirror. I floated there, gazing at the rapture of the light. The light was my soul. The recognition of this suspended me. I cannot escape my soul. I bumped into the mirror, again and again but I couldn't go through it. This was the end of the circle. I had come back to the source. All destinies are equal.

Dr. Marvin use to tell me that there was light at the end of the tunnel, and that all I had to do was keep moving forward and I would reach it. But I say, there is no light at the end of the tunnel; there is a mirror and you travel all that distance to find that the light you're chasing is inside yourself. And once you go inside and see it there is no doubt that you are sacred. There is no doubt that the universe within is infinite, and cannot be violated except by the refractions of the mind. There are no answers left unquestioned. There are no more boundaries or immunities or illusions. There is nothing to get out of life, you already have it all.

When I floated back to the prison hole, my body was not there. I flew up and down the rows of cells searching for it, and then headed for second aid. There, I hovered over a sheet-covered figure, which I didn't recognize to be my body, but it seemed to be the only vacant one lying around. I slipped inside, and it fit like mine, but it was cold and tired.

I opened my eyes to the gauzy haze of the sheet covering my face. I sat up, and tore the sheet off. I was naked, except for a tag that was tied on my toe. I stood on my wobbly blue legs and began to massage them back to pink. Wrapping the sheet back around myself, I hugged my body and it seemed to hug me back. I felt a new strength surging through me, a unity of body, mind, and spirit. I had been inverted and I understood the wisdom of the body now.

My body was hungry, and needed a shower. There was a clump of blood in my nose and I slowly walked over to the nurses station. Feeling my new feet, pressing into the gravity beneath the tiled floor, feeling a rising new voice in my throat, I called out to the aides, whose backs I could see through the glass office window. "I need some Kleenex!" I sang.

The aides looked horrified first, then came running out, and made me sit down.

"May I have some Kleenex?" I sang again.

They examined the tag that was tied on my toe, and told me that I was pronounced dead over an hour ago.

"Imagine that!" I crooned.

Dr. Marvin used to say that the mind controls the body and that I had to learn to control my mind. But I ask you, how can a mind be controlled if not through the power of a deeper mind? Hence, I say the deeper mind is within the molecular wisdom of the body. The deeper mind is the silent mind. The unquestioning mind. The deeper mind knows how to make the body breathe and it knows when it is time to cease breathing. The body has a mind of its own.

By telling the world about the reality of such species as the Sandman, I am able to help open the floodgates of perspective.

The Sandman is my brother, which was why I avoided discussing our relationship with Dr. Marvin. Dr. Marvin might have had both of us committed to institutions because of something he was unable to comprehend.

The Sandman came to me through synchronicity. A birthday wish. A need. The Sandman is my brother by means of mystical connections that I cannot begin to explain. But he is also my father, and Dr. Marvin, and BJ, and Rodger Badger, and Elvis, and Adam Sault, and God, and Buddha, and all of the karmic manifestations of the male ego present within us all. Each body, each mind, and each spirit is part male and part female, and when we fail to acknowledge this union within, then we will seek outside of ourselves for wholeness—and the universe will graciously supply the illusions.

The Sandman is not *quite* from beyond, he is in the heart of the artists. He is the door opener for those who dare to enter.

He used me indeed. He needed me to make the circle complete. The Sandman needed a body to restore the balance of the universal sphere of art. And my body, with so few immunities, slipped into its role as the Sandman's harbinger. We were tight, like black and white; the inseparable-impenetrable circle. The circle is only complete with an inside and an outside. Hence, the relationship of opposites is the perfect union.

Adam Sault gave me a gift, which until I began writing this book, I had not fully understood. He had told our drawing class this: "Always sign your work. When you sign it, then you are done with it. Whether you like it or not, you must learn to finish your work. Because you cannot move into the new picture until you admit being through with the old." He said that he knew of artists who'd had paintings hung on their walls for over twenty years, and that they would leap up in the middle of a social gathering to put yet another dab of paint on the canvas . . . another poem in the mail . . . another wall around the mind.

Pup asks me what my book is about and I tell her it's about breaking out of prison. She thinks I am writing a fairytale. But I ask you, how can I be a prisoner when my heart is expanding, when my perspective is inexhaustible? When you've lowered your immunities enough to let these words wobble around inside your head, where are the boundaries? Who is the prisoner?

That's all.